TAKAR

CONQUERED WORLD: BOOK ELEVEN

ELIN WYN

DAPHNE

"You look like a hungry Valorni," Annie laughed, watching as I went through my serving of noodles and thinly-sliced cuts of Luurizi meat.

"No," I protested with a mouthful, frowning as I eyed the tiny portion on her plate. "You're the one who's barely eating. Are you on a diet or something?"

"No, I just eat like a regular human being."

"It's not my fault the food is so damn good in here," I continued, barely stopping to breath as I devoured whatever was left on my plate. I exhaled deeply then, leaning back against my seat and feeling completely satisfied.

Biher's was a small restaurant located right between the main government building and Nyheim's hospital, where I'd had met Annie.

The restaurant was conveniently located between our two places of work, and we were both fans of the food there. Sure, food shortages sometimes wreaked havoc with the menu, but the place's atmosphere made up for that. Both aliens and humans ate here, no animosity between the two groups, and it felt like the perfect hiding spot from the growing tensions in the city.

"So, what's new?" I asked Annie, checking the holoscreen on the wall. I still had time before I had to be back at work, which meant I could pepper her with questions. There weren't any major surgeries planned for the afternoon, so I wouldn't be needed in the operating rooms.

"Same old," she smiled, fending off my question for the hundredth time. Luckily for me, she never grew tired of my non-stop questions. Curiosity was part of my DNA, after all, and Annie accepted that quirk of mine easily.

Of course, that just made me even more relentless in my pursuit of answers.

"Rocks, rocks, and then some more rocks. A thrilling day in a geologist's life."

"Oh, come on, Annie," I protested. "You gotta give me more than that. You're working under the mayor and General Rouhr. You must be working on something more interesting than just rocks. You could be analyzing the materials from the Xathi site, or you could be working on some geological samples that came on the *Vengeance*."

"It's nothing like that," she laughed, but I just kept pestering her with even more questions. That was my defining trait: whenever I started with the questions, I would never stop.

While it annoyed my parents to no end when I was growing up, it also ensured I had been curious enough to pursue a career in the neurosciences. Still, while work at the hospital was interesting—I helped out on surgeries while still conducting my research on the side—it wasn't enough for me. I always needed to know more about the world around me...and, after the aliens' arrival on the planet, that hunger for more had only grown exponentially.

"Alright, alright," she surrendered, holding both hands up. "I'm working on something you'd love, but I really can't say much."

"Is it a confidential project?"

"You know it."

"Crap. No clues?"

"Nope," she smiled. "The only thing I can say is that it's something so weird I'm pretty sure you'd love it."

I paused at that, going through all the possible

scenarios in my mind. There were a lot of areas where Annie's work could make a difference, but since she was working under the general, it had to be something of relevance to the government.

And it if wasn't connected to the Xathi or to something that had come from outside the planet...then it could only mean Annie was working on something that was happening right now, on this planet.

"You're working on the vines, aren't you?" I exclaimed, a wave of excitement running through me. The vines were probably one of the most interesting subjects a scientist could be studying right now, no doubt about that.

Too bad I was sitting on the sidelines, completely clueless to what was going on.

"How did you know?" she started, frowning as she realized I had seen through her. "I'm not supposed to talk about this with anyone, you know?"

"My lips are sealed," I said, pretending I was locking them up with an imaginary key I immediately flung off. "Just tell me what's the angle on this. Are you testing it for measurable signs of intelligence? Or even sentience? What kind of biometric readings are you using?"

"Look, I don't know much," she finally relented, a more serious expression on her face. "And even if I did, it's not like I'd be able to tell you. The only thing I might say is that the higher-ups call that...*thing*...the Puppet Master."

"The Puppet Master?"

"Lower your voice," she hissed, leaning forward and scanning the room with her eyes. No one seemed particularly concerned with our conversation, but I still mouthed an apology. "I don't wanna get in trouble. Everyone's already freaking out with how little they know, and the last thing they want is everyone in the city freaking out, too."

"Is there any reason for people to freak out?"

"Hello? Remember the way the vines tore the city apart? Or how we were trapped inside that dome? If that isn't enough for people to freak out about this Puppet Master, then I don't know what to tell you."

"Point taken," I nodded, a thousand thoughts already taking over my mind. Annie wasn't giving me much, but it was all so fascinating. "It's just that...well, there weren't that many casualties, were there? And the buildings that got destroyed, I somehow doubt they were targeted at random."

"What's that supposed to mean?" she asked, forehead creased.

"Well, the industrial precinct was the place with the most destroyed buildings. Do you think that's a coincidence? Because to me it looks like it happened deliberately. This thing, whatever it is, isn't just some dumb plant. There's real intelligence behind it."

Of course, I didn't have any proof to back what I was saying, but my gut was telling me that I was right. And, more often than not, my instincts had a tendency to be correct.

"That's...interesting," she hesitated over her words. "I hadn't considered that there could be a real pattern, although I agree with you that this thing has some kind of intelligence. Not that it matters much...there's little to no funding to conduct an investigation. And, to make matters worse, we're short-staffed. Everyone's just so damn busy trying to prevent more incidents, or at least ensuring we're ready for them."

"That's not enough," I said. "Prevention doesn't work without understanding. If we don't know what we're dealing with, how can we be prepared?"

"And you're asking me?" Annie smirked, rolling her eyes at me. "I don't have a general's insignia on my jacket, do I? Besides, I get their reasoning. Their priority is to ensure everyone's safety."

She continued to talk, defending her point of view, the general's point of view, whomever was working on this problem.

But I was no longer really processing anything she was saying.

Even though I gave her the occasional nod, my mind

was already working at a thousand miles an hour, trying to see this Puppet Master situation from all angles.

There were so many tests I could conduct, if given the chance.

Would any of my equipment work on the vines? What if I could get closer in, find the main plant? It was a plant, right?

If there was any intelligence, any real pattern, the vines were probably just an extension of this Puppet Master. And if that was the case, there had to be a nerve center of sorts. If I were to conduct any tests, I would have to find out its location.

Of course, that was impossible. My shoulders sank.

I wasn't invited to any of the government groups tackling the situation, and the government wasn't exactly sharing what they knew with the civilians. All I had were hypotheses and conjectures. And, if it weren't for Annie, I wouldn't even have that.

"Why the hell is this being kept a secret?" I said out loud, voicing my own thoughts. Annie just stopped whatever it was she was saying, her eyes wide with surprise, and then a frown took over her face.

"You weren't listening to me, were you?" she accused, and all I could do was shrug sheepishly.

"Sorry," I apologized, but I couldn't stop myself from hitting her with a follow-up question. "But, seriously, why doesn't the government share what they know? Maybe not to the civilians, but there are a lot of scientists in the city that could help."

"The timing just isn't that great," Annie sighed. "With all the anti-alien sentiment going around, the general probably feels it's better not to stir the pot. I mean, how easy would it be for the anti-alien groups to say this Puppet Master is the aliens' fault?"

"True," I agreed.

"One step at a time, I guess," she shrugged. "The general has already set up the public inquiry office, so that's something."

"The inquiry office..." I repeated, remembering something I had seen on the holonews a few days ago. "The project spearheaded by that woman, what was here name, Stacy something?"

"Stasia. Stasia Cole. She used to work here, can you believe it? She proposed it as a way to bridge the communication gap between the aliens and the humans. I'm not sure if it'll work, though. People are stubborn, and the anti-alien propaganda is strong."

"People will see the light," I said, choosing to believe most people would see through the propaganda.

"Well, some people are actually going to the office," she shrugged, "although I guess most of them just go there to complain."

"Maybe someone should go there to ask questions

instead of complaints," I mused, an idea already brewing inside my head.

Annie just pursed her lips, her forehead creasing with concern.

"Don't do anything stupid, Daphne."

"Me?" I laughed. "Never!"

TAKAR

I woke up in darkness, which wasn't terribly unusual. I almost always woke up well before the sun painted the sky. Today, however, was darker than others. It was a combination of the heavy clouds bringing down the nonstop gentle rain since yesterday, and my mood. Today, I was assigned to be "Complaint Officer." A low growl escaped my lips.

There was only one light on in the apartment, the one for the cleansing room, and it was something small that plugged into the electrical socket.

No matter how old we grew, Rokul still needed at least that light on. He could sleep in utter darkness, but when it was time to use the cleansing room, if he didn't have some sort of light on, he'd curse and fumble around in the dark, occasionally missing the mark and making a mess.

My brother was by far the most unusual person I had ever met. Even now, with Tella part of his life—and occupying his bed—he was still the same person he had been while we were growing up.

I quietly tiptoed past their room on my way to the cleansing room. Once inside, I closed the door, turned on the wall light, and went about my morning routine.

As I washed myself in the shower, I thought about the inquiry office that General Rouhr had created in order to appease the whiney humans. Granted, not all of them were annoying crybabies, but why did we have to listen to their complaints and give them either answers or advice on how to deal with those complaints…what was the point? All the humans needed to do was trust that we were doing what was right.

They had never faced the Xathi before, they didn't know what kind of cleanup was involved after a Xathi attack. *Where did he put my toothpaste?* Of course, *he put it* there. We were doing what was necessary, why couldn't they just accept that?

Why should they, as a collective, know as much as we did? I didn't know everything that the general did, and I didn't want to know. Back in the war, before the rift, I didn't know what the War Council did and that was fine with me. If I had a complaint, *spit, rinse, spit,* I dealt with it myself or learned to accept that there were just things I didn't like.

I cleaned up after myself, making sure the cleansing room, or bathroom, was as clean as it was before I used it.

There was light streaming out from under Rokul and Tella's door. "Morning," I said as I walked by.

"Morning," I heard Tella groan, then she yelped and started cursing at Rokul as he laughed. He must have pinched her again. He had started doing that fairly often lately, and it was going to get him in trouble.

I made myself a simple breakfast of eggs, bacon, and something Tella called oatmeal. It tasted better than the breakfast gruel I used to eat on the ship, so I was content. As the couple came to join me in the kitchen, I was already finishing off my last bite.

"You're on Complaint Officer duty, right?" Rokul asked, which put me into an even sourer mood. To match my mood, thunder clapped outside and the rain intensified slightly.

"Yes," I grumbled as I rose from the table to wash my plate.

"Ooh, Stuffy is grumpy today," Tella teased, using the nickname for me that she had fashioned. "Come on, it's not that bad. You just have to sit down and pretend to listen to people. I do it with you two every day."

"Hey!" Rokul exclaimed in mock indignation.

While they laughed, I gathered my gear, double checked my weaponry to ensure that it was properly cleaned, loaded, and stored, then bid them good-day. The rain was still gentle, but annoyingly cold. It was a sign that the seasons were about to change. I wondered what winter on Ankau would look like, or if the planet was in a perpetual state of late spring/early summer.

I ensured my pack was closed and that my rifle was covered, then stepped out into the rain. I marched to the general's office building, only to be greeted by a line of humans waiting outside...already. I stepped into the building, dried myself off with one of the many towels Tobias had placed by the door, and headed to the room that General Rouhr had specifically set aside for human complaints and named it with a sign, subtitled, "Complaints and Redress".

The room itself was fairly simple, and comfortable by human standards. There was a big wooden desk with an overly comfortable chair for me to sit in, three other semi-comfortable chairs arranged in front of the desk, a couch, and in a corner, a small table with things to do for children.

I looked over the list of issues that were still unanswered from the day before, resigned myself to having to deal with people complaining about not getting their complaints dealt with, and buzzed Tobias. "Let them in," I said dejectedly.

Over the next several hours, I listened to complaints about the lack of food, how bland the simulated food was, questions about why we hadn't fixed a certain neighborhood yet, at least two people with nothing better to do than simply throw insults at me, and a complaint about the lack of suitable technology at one of the schools.

Alright. The last one was something I would be interested in doing something about.

Nothing was more important than learning. Learning leads to knowledge, which led to proper preparedness, which led to not getting caught by surprise and being capable of completing whatever task needed to be completed.

I made that one a priority and sent it off to Tu'ver, Sylor, and Iq'her. They were collectively in charge of trying to improve the technology of the city.

Finally, there was one more person…a woman by the name of Daphne March. Her 'complaint' was that she was nervous about the fate of her city. *Well, if these damn humans would just trust us to know what was best and allow us to handle our responsibilities, there would be nothing to be nervous about. These rekking idiots that are part of the 'anti-alien' group just needed to shut the rekk up and stay out of our way. We would leave soon enough.*

If we could.

Of course, no matter what my thoughts were, the likelihood of us leaving was evaporating more and more every day. Too many of us were getting close to the humans, developing friendships and relationships with them. I was certain that Vrehx and Rouhr would stay here if we had the chance to leave.

I worried that Rokul would stay, as well.

I looked up as this Daphne person entered the room. A petite brunette, she looked around every corner, curiosity lighting her eyes.

Her distraction gave me a moment to collect myself. It seemed unthinkable that anyone would be able to look as attractive as she did in a war-ravaged city. She had her hair tied up in what was commonly referred to as a top-knot, but stray strands fell to soften the look. My hand itched to push the silky strands back behind her ear.

I fought the feeling, realizing the eager smile on her face seemed very out of place for someone that was 'nervous.'

"How can I help you, Miss March?" I asked in my most professional voice, not really caring what her response was going to be as I ran my gaze up and down her form.

She was voluptuous and curvy and in my mind one of the prettiest humans I had ever laid eyes upon.

Annoyed at myself for being distracted, I refocused on the datapad before me.

She fairly bounced across the room and into one of the chairs across from me. She seemed to be far too happy to be here.

"Hi. I was wondering if you could tell me about the Puppet Master."

My head snapped up from my perusal of my paperwork. She sat there, smiling at me.

"I'm sorry," I said trying to focus. "I was under the impression that you were here to discuss your nervousness about the city."

"Yeah, I know," she replied, her voice far too energetic and peppy. "I lied. I'm really here to get more information about whatever that thing is that's responsible for the plants."

This was entirely too disconcerting. She wasn't afraid. She was interested.

About something she shouldn't know anything about.

I needed to know how much she knew already, so I asked her.

That was possibly a mistake.

She talked, and talked, and talked. Sometimes her sentences were about what she knew, but most of the time they were about what her thoughts were of it and what she thought those thoughts meant. It was like listening to Axtin go on and on about one of his battles.

As of Axtin's latest telling of how he saved Leena from the Xathi ship, he destroyed nearly a hundred Xathi with his bare hands and that infernal hammer of his.

Daphne finally stopped talking. "So?" she asked, proving me a liar on the 'stopped talking' part. "What can you tell me?"

"I can tell you that we're doing the best we can to contain the situation and determine a proper course of action," I answered.

"But what course of action are you taking? Do you know if the Puppet Master is intelligent? Can it talk? Have you tried communicating with it? What if we can't fix things?" She threw out so many questions, I lost track of what she was saying.

"Why did you lie about your concerns?" I asked as a way of stopping her.

She shrugged and smiled at me. "I didn't think you'd tell me anything if I just asked outright."

"I see. Well, in regard to the Puppet Master, it is a creature that we are currently studying and determining the best course of action on how to deal with it," I explained. "We are looking into new ways to save the vegetation that we all use." I held up my hand to stop her from talking any more. "I will pass on your concerns to the city leaders in an attempt to find more information. Thank you for expressing your concerns and I hope your day improves."

"But, what about…"

"Ma'am, I must apologize, but I have other people that I need to speak with. It's time to go," I said as I stood up and made my way to the door. I held it open for her as she left. She opened her mouth to say something, but I closed the door and returned to the desk.

I wondered who she had talked to before me.

And when I'd get the chance to talk to her again.

DAPHNE

Who knew?

Apparently, the guy in charge of communicating with the humans decided *not* to communicate. I hadn't known what to expect when I sat across that Skotan, but I sure as hell hadn't thought I'd leave the inquiry office in a state of pure annoyance.

He had fed me nothing but bullshit answers, all of them designed to placate me. Sure, I had come out swinging, but that approach had never failed me before. I had even turned up my charm and used my 'pretty-please' smile.

"Stupid Skotan," I grumbled, feeling completely deflated. Annie had teased me with what was one of the biggest scientific mysteries in the planet, and I had met a brick wall the moment I decided to learn more.

Sure, a handsome-as-all-hell brick wall. Even if he was grumpy.

Fantastic.

"Did you just call me stupid?" Bale muttered from his corner of the lab, even though he didn't look away from his computer screen. Smart and competent, he was a lanky man in his thirties whose dream life seemed to involve nothing but a basket of snacks and a computer screen. That didn't bother me at all, especially since I needed him in front of a computer whenever he was around.

"No, sorry," I chuckled nervously. "I was just thinking out loud."

"Thinking of stupid people?" he continued, the sound of his fingers hitting the keyboard over and over again echoing throughout the lab. Even though he was what some would call socially awkward, I had always gotten along with him. On paper, he was my assistant, but our relationship was one of equals.

"Actually, yeah," I sighed, looking away from my computer. I had been going through some neurological holoscans for the past couple of hours, but it was hard to concentrate with the Puppet Master firmly occupying all of my thoughts. "I was just at that inquiry office the government set up and—"

"You went there?" He cut me short, finally looking away from his computer. He had his eyebrows arched, almost as if I had just said something terribly stupid. "You know that's just a PR stunt, don't you? As if government would ever be transparent."

"Don't tell me you've been listening to that anti-alien propaganda."

"Me?" he laughed. "Please, Daphne. I couldn't care less about the aliens. I just think that it doesn't matter who's in charge. Aliens, humans…at the end of the day, it's all the same."

"Didn't know you were so anti-system," I said.

"How do you think I ended up as your assistant?" He smirked, folding his arms over his chest and swiveling around in his chair so that he could face me. "Because I can tell you, my childhood dream wasn't to be some glorified IT guy."

"You're not an IT guy," I frowned. "You're helping me with important neurological research, and your tech savvy is essential. I wouldn't be able to code all the equipment by myself."

"And that's why I'm here," he nodded. "Your faithful sidekick."

"But if you don't like it…what exactly are you doing here?" I had to admit I was confused. I didn't know much about Bale's personal life, and had always assumed his studies had led him to a position in the hospital.

"It's not that I don't like it," he shrugged. "I actually

do. But when I first started out in here…let's just say I had no other option. At least, according to the judge."

"The judge?"

"Yeah," he smiled sardonically. "Community service, if you can believe it. One entire month of unpaid work here at the hospital. I restructured all the network and updated the IT systems in my first week, and by then nobody really knew what to do with me. And since you needed an assistant, I guess they just decided to send me your way."

"But you've been with me for more than a month," I said, frowning. "You've been here for a lot longer than that."

"I guess I enjoy working with you," he said casually, already turning his attention back to the screen. When I realized he wasn't going to tell me anything else, my curious side immediately came alive.

"Hang on," I said, pushing my chair back and getting to my feet. "You can't just hit me with that and then not tell the rest of the story. What's up with you doing community service?"

"Is it that hard to guess?" He laughed, jutting his chin to point at the computer screen in front of him. "Let's just say I have a way with computers, and that some people are willing to pay for information…the kind of information I can easily get."

"You're a hacker?" I asked him, not sure of what to make of it. I knew he was somewhat reclusive and had a quirky personality, but had never guessed he could be a criminal.

"You make it sound like I'm some super-villain," he laughed once more. "Mostly I was hired by people that weren't sure if their spouses were being faithful. They *needed* to know what their better half was doing whenever they weren't around. Spoiler: most people didn't like the information I uncovered. They all paid, though, so I'm not complaining. Well, most of them."

"You got caught doing that?"

"Eh, well," he hesitated, scratching his chin. "More or less. It was before the Xathi invasion, and I was working for some guy that thought his wife was cheating on him. She wasn't, actually, but the guy didn't believe me…and he went straight to the authorities and told them I was some sort of super-hacker. Just so he wouldn't have to pay me, if you can believe it. Two Nyheim city guards showed up on my doorstep, and they dragged my ass to the courthouse. One week later and I had a new desk, right in the hospital's basement. That's when the Xathi attack happened and I've been here ever since."

"That's quite a story," I told him, not knowing what else to say. I didn't exactly approve of his previous career, but it wasn't as if he had been a hardened criminal. Besides, it seemed he had a special set of skills that could be very useful...

"Well, maybe one day I'll write a book," he smiled, his eyes already focused on the lines of code that littered his computer screen. His fingers flew over his keyboard as he worked, and I started formulating a plan.

"Why hasn't the government grabbed you to help with the rebuilding process," I wondered. "Reassigned you somewhere else?"

He shrugged, eyes still on the screen. "It's possible I removed a bit of my past from my files, when everything was messed up after the attack. It's possible no one knows I'm here."

Interesting.

And possibly useful.

All I needed was for Bale to cooperate.

"What if I told you I need some information?" I blurted out, and held my breath as his fingers stopped. With one eyebrow cocked, he swiveled his chair around once more.

"I'm not sure if I feel comfortable snooping on your boyfriend," he said, and I could tell he was surprised I had made such a request.

"I don't have a boyfriend," I blushed, wetting my lips

with the tip of my tongue. "All I want is some information about the vines."

"The vines?" he repeated, his expression one of confusion. "Was that why you went to the inquiry office? Did you think anyone there would share their research with you?"

"Well..."

"God, Daphne," he smiled. "These guys would cut an arm off before they revealed what's on the menu in the officers' dining hall. Something like the vines...yeah, that information would be as confidential as it gets."

"And would confidential be a problem for you?" I asked, biting on the corner of my lip. I didn't like it that I was asking Bale to break the law on my behalf, but if he was any good...well, this was an opportunity that was simply too good for me to pass up.

If it was possible I could help with this puzzle, I wanted to. But first, I needed to know what they knew.

If I had to be a rebel, then so be it.

"Let's be clear...are you asking me to hack into the government's servers?"

"Yeah?"

"Shit," he laughed, running one hand through his hair. He drummed his fingers against his thigh, an expression that I could only describe as a blend of focus and excitement showing on his face. "I didn't think you were the kind of person to ignore the rules. I'm impressed."

"All in the name of science," I beamed, excited that Bale seemed to be playing along with me. "Only in the name of science, really. So, do you think you can do it? I don't know if it helps, but they're calling the vines…the Puppet Master."

"That's ominous," he said. "But it helps me to know what to look for." He hesitated for a moment, weighing his options, and then gave me a serious nod. "Alright, I'll do it for you. Just, uh, don't tell anyone."

"My lips are sealed," I told him, my stomach tightening a bit when I remembered I'd promised Annie the same thing. But she was a scientist, too. She'd understand the need to dig into this.

Maybe.

Pushing my chair across the lab, I then sat beside Bale, my heart racing at a hundred miles an hour.

"Alright," he grunted and started minimizing the windows on his screen and opening a new one. He tapped a few keys, and then hesitated, his lips pursed as he looked at the weird characters that had filled up the screen. "Seems like some of the information is written in Skotan. I might get into the servers, but I don't know if we'll be able to translate the information."

"Most of that should be a direct translation of the reports submitted by the human scientists," I whispered, thinking feverishly. "What if, instead of grabbing the information the aliens are using...you grab the original reports the scientists have submitted?"

"That might work," he nodded, his fingers working fast. I don't think he even blinked as lines of code ran across the screen, his eyes burning with excitement. After almost an hour, he leaned back in his chair and turned to me. "Done. I redirected most of the reports toward us but..."

"But?"

"Well, apparently no one knows that much about this Puppet Master. There are a lot of written reports, but the information there doesn't seem to be that conclusive. They're in the dark."

"That's odd," I muttered, even though I grabbed my datapad from my lab coat all the same. "Can you transfer whatever information you got to my 'pad?"

"Done," he grinned, tapping his keyboard just once.

"And make sure there's no trace of us in their servers."

"Please, Daphne," he laughed. "You didn't even need to ask."

"You're the best." Jumping up to my feet, I placed my datapad inside my lab coat once more. Wrapping my arms around Bale, I hugged him tightly. "I owe you one."

"You sure do."

"I'm going to take the rest of the afternoon off," I continued, already anxious to dig deeper into the Puppet Master. Even if the information we had stolen wasn't much, it was a start, all the same.

"There's someone I need to talk to."

TAKAR

As much as I would have loved it for Daphne to have been my last visitor of the morning, she wasn't. To be fair, I would not be complaining as much if Daphne had come in again, even to ask about classified matters.

Especially with the tight clothes she had been wearing. I don't know if I'd listen to her complaints any more, but I'd have an appealing sight to behold.

Unfortunately, there was still a line outside. One that I had forgotten about in interacting with the lovely Daphne.

"Tobias?" I called over the desk-to-desk comm.

"How can I help you, Takar?" came the answer.

"What time is it?" I asked.

I knew the time, I just hoped that somehow all my instruments were wrong.

Surely my shift was over…

"Since you worked through lunch, your brother has left a message for you to take a break and meet him at the range instead.," he told me.

"Very well," I said. Leave it to Rokul to make lunch about training instead of lunch. I didn't remember how many times I had explained to him that, for people like him and me, with our body size and types, food was a requirement. There were few times that we would be able to bypass a meal before we began to feel the negative effects. "Please tell the people outside that I am going to lunch."

"They won't be happy," he said back, his tone low. There must have been people inside the building waiting to see me.

"Not my issue," I said matter-of-factly. "If they want to voice a complaint, they can either wait until I return or come back tomorrow." With that, I turned the comm off and left the office. I walked right out the front, right past all the people waiting in line—not nearly as many as this morning, but still an annoying number—and ignored their glares as I left the building.

When I walked out the door, I turned to my right, walked one block down the road, then turned right again. At the end of the street was the barracks, and at the back of the barracks was the target range.

And there was Rokul, massive smile on his face, waiting for me. "Ho, Takar!" he called out to me, waving at me. He was a walking tree trunk, a little like some of the strange trees grown on this world actually, yet he was a bit smaller than me.

We were the same height, and he was the older by a year, but I had the bigger muscle mass, and the bigger cranial capacity. Where Rokul was the more social of the two of us, I was the more intellectual, even if I didn't come across as a pretentious prick like Sylor.

"Ho, brother," I called back. "How many times do I have to explain to you that food is a necessity?"

He winked at me. "Yeah, yeah, and how many times do I need to tell you that we can deal without food once in a while. We need to keep up our training."

"There are few that are better shots than us, brother," I said, hopping the short fence that separated the walkway from the range and walking up to him.

He shrugged.

I rolled my eyes. "Basically, you're using this as an excuse to shoot a gun and try to make fun of me for the duty that I pulled."

"You know me so well," he laughed as he tossed me a blaster and three clips.

I couldn't help but join in the laughter as we walked

over to our firing bays. "So, best of three?" he asked as he set his weapon down and reached for the protective eyewear.

"Accuracy or speed?" I asked. I actually felt good at the moment, even if I didn't show it.

"Both?" he smiled as he handed me my target.

I smirked. "Ah, you're in the mood to lose today."

"Whatever," he waved me off. "Are you ready?"

"In a moment," I answered. I put on my eyewear, placed my weapon and clips on the small counter, and took four deep breaths. I then walked back to the fence with Rokul. "On three, or on your usual two-and-a-half?"

He feigned shock, his mouth overdramatically open. "Ah, me? Cheat? When?"

"The last time we did this," I said.

"Eh," he laughed. "On three...a real three."

"Good." I took a deep breath and got myself ready.

"One." I wasn't going to lose to him, not today.

"Two." I dug my foot in and tensed myself.

"THREE!" We launched at the same time and sprinted towards our weapons. Rokul, in his usual immature fashion, reached out towards me in an attempt to slow me down.

"Not this time, brother," I yelled back as I swatted his hand away. We reached our shooting positions at the same time. I grabbed my gun, snapped a clip into it, chambered a round, and took aim.

Rokul was the first to fire by half a heartbeat. I cleaned out the fifteen rounds in my clip, released it, snapped the next clip in, and cleaned it out. I was ahead of my brother going into the third clip.

I released my clip, set the gun down quickly, and stepped back...one step before Rokul.

"Fine," he huffed. "You were faster, but I'm pretty sure I was more accurate." I pushed him away with a laugh. We brought our targets back in and did a quick count.

Skrell. He beat me by one shot. "Well," I said. "It's been a long time since we've tied."

"What are you talking about? Accuracy is more important than speed," he argued. "That means I win."

I laughed again. "Fine, you win," I conceded.

"At least you're smiling and laughing," he said. When I flashed him a look, he explained. "I've heard complaints about the 'charmer' in the office this morning."

I rolled my eyes and let out a sigh. I grabbed my clips and gun. "Why should I care what those people say?"

"Uh, because we work with those people and we're trying to fix what we broke?" Rokul answered.

"Brother," I said in anger. "I did not train and work

so I could listen to people whine. I did not participate in two wars so I could listen to people complain. I did not sign up to be in customer service."

"I know, but it's not that bad. It's only once every two weeks," he argued. "Besides, those are good for you."

"How?" I snapped.

"They might just turn you into a decent person," he said, his mouth hanging open in mock horror. I threw a clip at him. He ducked and took off running, his laughter trailing behind like a wisp of smoke.

We turned in our weapons and sat down to eat. I was honestly surprised he had remembered to get the food this time. I was cycling through the daily reports on my tablet when a warning light went off.

"What's that?" my brother asked through a mouthful of food.

"Someone is trying to hack into our system," I said. His eyes bugged out and he stopped chewing.

"Really?" he said, tiny particles of food falling from his mouth as he spoke.

"Learn to eat," I snapped, mind focused on the intrusion. "We need to talk to General Rouhr." He nodded and grabbed his meal, something he had ordered called a burger, and mine, as well.

"Here," he said as he shoved my burger at me. "You're the one always saying food is important. Eat."

I devoured my food in three bites as we jogged back to the office. Again, I ignored the line waiting for me and went right to Tobias. "The general?" I asked, knowing Tobias would always be aware of Rouhr's current location.

He said nothing, but he did point downstairs. I knew where he would be. Under the main floor of the building were the computer servers and cool storage. If I had gotten the alarm notice, then he had, as well.

We rushed down and found him in the main server room with three techs, already working on the issue.

"Any information, sir?" I asked as we walked in.

"Nothing yet," he said without looking up. He was leaning over the chair of one of the techs, looking at what had been found. "All we know is someone is trying to hack into the system from the hospital."

With a nod, I looked at the tech to my left. "Pull up hospital employment records." He immediately turned in his chair and began typing on his keyboard. "Bring up pictures if they're available," I added.

It didn't take long.

The tech began cycling through the records of everyone that worked at the hospital; doctors, nurses, techs, scientists, lab personnel, janitors, cooks. Then, there was a picture that caught my attention.

"Wait. Go back…more…more…there, that one!" I pointed at the screen. "I know her."

"You do?" Rouhr asked.

"Yes, sir. She was one of the people in line for the complaint office this morning," I explained. There was no way I could ever forget that face. Or that body.

He sighed. "You know I hate it when my soldiers call it that, but that's beside the point. What was she concerned with?"

"She came in under the pretense of being nervous over what the direction of the city was, but then she tried pressing me for information about the Puppet Master," I answered. "She knew about it by name."

"Fantastic. Did you tell her anything?" he asked.

I shook my head. "No, sir. Standard rote answers."

"Good," he breathed a sigh of relief. "If she is part of this anti-alien group that seems to be gaining momentum and size, then we need to find out why she was interested."

"I agree," I said.

"Well, good, because you're the one that's going to look for her," he said with a smile.

Of course I was. "Yes, sir. Permission to make my brother go with me?"

"What? Why do I have to be part of this?" Rokul blurted.

Rouhr laughed. "Granted. Go."

We left the office building and made our way to the hospital.

"I hate you, you know that?" Rokul grinned as he punched me in my shoulder.

"Eh, you know you love the work," I shot back, then started sprinting to the hospital.

Rokul let out a string of curses behind me as he tried to catch up.

And I wondered what the lovely Daphne had to do with this.

DAPHNE

"What are you doing here?" Annie asked me as I strolled inside her lab. She looked up from the samples that littered her work bench, both hands on her hips.

"What?" I smiled sheepishly. "Don't tell me I can't visit my good friend whenever the mood strikes."

"We just had lunch yesterday," she said, narrowing her eyes as her expression turned into a suspicious one. "Please, don't tell me you've come to ask more questions."

"Me? Please."

"So, I'm right. You have more questions."

"Yeah," I laughed, looking around her lab to ensure we were alone. "I just couldn't stop thinking about the Puppet Master. I'm pretty sure we're dealing with an intelligent life form. And, even though the general believes the Puppet Master's hostile toward us, I have my doubts."

"And what do you know about what the general believes?" she asked me, but all I could offer her was a shrug.

As much as I trusted Annie, I probably shouldn't tell her I had enlisted the help of my assistant to hack into the government's servers.

"It's just a guess, really."

"Just a guess, huh?"

"Yeah, and I have a lot more guesses," I smiled, feeling so excited I didn't even know if I should remain standing up or sit down. My body was brimming with energy, and my synapses seemed to be firing at the speed of light. "I know the government isn't exactly hiring, but I think I'd be able to help. I have a lot of ideas about how we can conduct research and—"

"Whoa, slow down," Annie laughed. "The general has a lot of experts working on it. I know you just want to help but—"

"Not just help," I cut her short. "I want to do more. I want to solve this."

"You make it sound easy."

"No," I corrected her, "I just make it sound *fun*. How did you get a job here, Annie? There must be a way for me to secure a position here."

"If only it were that easy," she sighed. "I know you're good at what you do, but we're not exactly hiring, not with all the anti-alien groups making a fuss. If I had to guess, the general is worried that we might unwittingly hire a saboteur. And, since we don't really know what we're dealing with, he's being cautious letting people in on our research."

"There must be a way."

"I really wish I could help you, Daphne," she continued, smiling kindly. "But there's not much I can do. I can recommend you to General Rouhr, but he works on his own schedule, with his own priorities. Even my position here...I just got it out of pure luck. I mean, my boss facilitated a team-up, but I only managed to stay in here because of the samples I took at the crater."

"Samples?"

"Yeah," she nodded. "At the Xathi site. The whole place was the epicenter for a lot of seismic activity in the region. They didn't allow me to go there, so I just snuck out and..." She trailed off, probably realizing she wasn't supposed to be sharing any of that with me.

"A crater?" I asked her, feeling even more excited than before. Could there be a connection to the Puppet Master? The vines had come from the underground, so seismic activity would suggest a connection. Maybe if I could get to the crater, I'd be able to find out more.

"Okay, Daphne," she shook her head, regret burning in her eyes. "You're going to forget I told you any of that. I don't want to get in trouble and, more than that, I don't want *you* to get in trouble."

"I just—"

"Look, I'm serious," she interrupted me. "I want you to promise me you won't do anything stupid, illegal, dangerous...or any combination of those three."

"I…fine. I promise," I said, and I really meant it.

At least to an extent.

After all, the only illegal thing I did had happened before this promise, and I was pretty sure that a trip to the crater was everything but stupid. As for the 'not doing anything dangerous' part...well, I intended to be careful, and that would have to suffice.

"I'm serious, Daphne," she insisted, looking at me sternly.

"Don't worry." Taking a step toward her, I went on tiptoes and kissed her forehead. "I'll behave."

"You better."

"Always," I laughed, already walking out of her lab. The moment I was out of the building I started making my way back toward the hospital.

Except, instead of going straight to the main building, I continued down the road and toward the massive storage building on the other end of the complex.

Being a reputable neuroscientist at Nyheim Hospital had its perks, and one of those perks was security clearance. All I needed to do was show my ID to the guards at the gate and they waved me in like it was nothing. I made my way through the parking lot and toward the main entrance, opening the door by swiping my ID across the panel on the wall. The circuitry lit up a bright green, and the massive door slid up into its partition.

The lights came on the moment I stepped inside the massive warehouse, shelves of medical equipment going from one end of the building to the other. The whole place was automated, so I headed toward one of the electronic terminals and logged into the system.

As I started entering my equipment requests into the terminal, Annie's words echoed inside my head.

I had convinced myself I wasn't breaking the promise I had made, but...well, that was just some bullshit I had spun in order not to feel guilty about lying.

Lying to my best friend.

But, hell, this was important.

Besides, it wasn't like anybody had to know. One quick trip to the crater, coordinates helpfully noted in the reports, just so I could look around and collect some samples, and then I'd be back before anybody noticed a thing. It wasn't ideal, but what was I to do? I couldn't do any official research, so this was my only available option.

And maybe I'd have enough to present some options to the general or his staff. Convince them I should be on the team.

Not the grumpy Skotan from this morning, though. That chiseled jaw and the rippling muscles might intrigue me, but he was far too interested in following the rules for my taste.

Even if he might be worth one, little taste...

"Request processed," an electronic voice announced, startling me from my increasingly off-topic thoughts, when the automatic warehouse bots were done with collecting the equipment I needed. I went to the delivery room to grab the things I would need, and sighed as I watched it all laid out on the table. Most of the equipment wasn't state-of-the-art, but there wasn't much I could do about that.

In order not to trigger a review by one of my supervisors, I had to request only equipment I knew to be outdated or that hadn't gone through the proper maintenance procedures.

Still, I wasn't going to let that stop me.

Placing all the gear inside my bag, I took a deep breath and marched out of the warehouse. I was feeling slightly nervous. A little guilty.

But more than that, I was elated. Science required

its disciples to rebel against the authorities from time to time, and that was exactly what I intended to. Besides, if everything went according to plan, there was a possibility I'd collect enough information to land me a spot on the government's research team.

And there I could really help out.

But first things first.

Holding up my datapad in front of my face, I make a call.

"Daphne? Finally found enough time in your schedule to call your worried parents?" my mother teased me, pushing her glasses up the bridge of her nose.

"Well, actually…" I hesitated, smiling sheepishly. "I need to ask you for a favor."

TAKAR

The rain that had stopped before lunch yesterday had returned during the night.

This time, it hadn't been a gentle rain, as the lightning cracked and thunder crashed for hours. The heavy winds brought the rain down in force, pinging off the metal roof of the apartment like gunfire.

I slept like a newborn.

That following morning, I awoke to silence. Either the storm had passed or it was simply a short lull. A quick glance out the window showed stars in the sky above us. Without a care, I went about my morning business.

I wasn't on desk duty today.

Instead, I was going to be on patrol. We had the

anti-alien groups to look out for as well as further attacks from the Puppet Master.

Patrol was so much better than desk duty. Patrol meant movement. It meant conversations with people that had similar experiences. It meant being able to actually *do* something.

Patrol meant I could walk away from the humans that annoyed me.

As I ate, and was forced to listen to my brother and Tella do their morning...*business*...then clean up afterwards, I thought about how yesterday had ended.

Rokul and I had left the office and raced to the hospital. He complained the entire time, saying that I had cheated during our race.

It wasn't my fault that he wasn't fast enough to catch me. When we arrived at the hospital, we proceeded to the security desk. The guard on duty was a bit apprehensive at the prospect of helping us at first, but he relented.

We double checked personnel files to find out that Daphne worked in one of the advanced labs.

However, according to hospital records, no one had been working in any of the labs that day. The labs held the only computers in the hospital that were advanced enough to hack into *Vengeance's* systems.

Not satisfied with the information we received from the security office, we went asking around. No one could recall having seen Daphne, at least not for very long. Someone said that they had seen Daphne come in, but then she left soon afterwards.

No one knew where she was.

No one knew about anyone else who had been in the labs, or might be able to breach our systems.

Nothing.

That had resulted in my being forced to return to the complaint office where, of course, I was forced to listen to complaints and concerns, made worse now that they had to wait for so long to have someone to complain to.

That had been yesterday.

Yesterday had been awful.

Today would be much better.

This morning, I was going on patrol with my brother. If we found Daphne, we would deal with her. If we didn't, fine, at least I didn't have to listen to people moan and groan about things they didn't need to worry about.

"Did you save any food for us?" Rokul asked as he followed Tella into the kitchen, giving her a playful slap on the butt as he sat down next to me at the counter. She let out a small yelp, smacked him in the head, and went to fix them breakfast.

I shook my head. "I always leave food for you. Must

you insist on serenading me with your exploits in the morning?"

I could see Tella blush slightly. Rokul chuckled and had the grace to look at least a little embarrassed. "Ah, you heard that, huh?"

I looked at him as if he was an idiot. "I think the neighbors, both next to us, across from us, and under us, heard you two."

They both chuckled. "At least we didn't break anything this time," Tella snickered as she walked to the cool-box.

I rolled my eyes as I shook my head. "You two are incorrigible," I sighed. "I'm getting ready for work. Let me know when you care enough to join me."

"Whoa, easy little brother," my brother said as he held up his hands. "You know I'm good for work. Give me a few minutes to eat and grab my gear."

I merely nodded and walked away. I went to my room, grabbed my gear, and double checked it. When I was satisfied, I made my way to the common area of the apartment. Rokul was waiting for me. When he saw me, he smiled.

"I had my gear prepped last night," he said. "You ready?"

At my nod, he gave Tella a kiss and we left.

"So," he started. "What do you want to do today?"

I arched an eyebrow. "We're on patrol duty today. What could you possibly mean?"

"Well, yeah, I know we're on patrol duty today," he said. "But we don't always have to patrol the same way. I was just wondering where you wanted to patrol."

"Ah," I said in response. "I'm perfectly fine with our standard patrol pattern."

"Of course, you are," my brother said dejectedly. "You and your habits."

I was getting ready to respond when a familiar human came rushing up to us.

I looked over to see Annie pull up in front of us, out of breath. After a quick moment, she managed to get her words out. "Do you know where General Rouhr is? I need to talk to him, it's really important."

Well, since she didn't need us, I was perfectly content with sending her on her way. I opened my mouth to give her directions to where Rouhr was going to be today, but my brother interrupted me. "What's the matter?"

"It's my friend Daphne," she started. "I think she's missing."

My brother and I both perked up at the mention of her name. This was the same woman we had been looking for yesterday. "Missing? Are you sure?" I asked.

She nodded. "Mm-hmm. She was asking me a

bunch of questions about the Puppet Master yesterday, then she just vanished."

I took a step closer to Annie. "Tell me everything," I ordered.

She hesitated slightly, her eyebrows raised at my exuberance. "Well, she was interested in what the mental intelligence of the Puppet Master was. She was surprised that none of us ever looked into figuring out how smart the thing was. Then, she went to talk to you," she nodded in my direction, "and after that, I don't know."

"Why was she interested in the creature's intelligence?" I asked.

She shrugged. "Well, the more I think about it, the more it makes sense. Tella and I both think that this thing has some level of sentience. It would explain how the attacks weren't focused on actually hurting people, but just causing damage, and how the dome surrounded the town without destroying it." Then she stopped to think for a moment. "Actually, now that I think about it, it would also explain why we were able to take the dome down without any sort of retaliation."

"So, you're saying that this thing is smart and this friend of yours was interested in finding out how smart?" my brother asked.

She nodded. "That's why I need to find the general. I need to find her."

"Any idea where she could have gone?" I asked.

She shrugged. "I'm not sure. All I know is that I can't get hold of her and her parents' hovercraft is gone."

I was still a little concerned about where the woman could have gone, but I was beginning to doubt it was anything bad. "Maybe she left to go get something, or perhaps she went somewhere to take some time off," I suggested.

"No, Daphne isn't the type to just take off without telling people," Annie argued. "I'm worried she's gone off and done something stupid."

"Like what?" Rokul asked.

"Well," Annie started, looking a bit embarrassed. "When we were talking yesterday, I may have mentioned how I first came into contact with the Puppet Master. You know, how I checked out the crater it had created?"

Everything clicked into place. Daphne was interested in the intelligence of this creature. She had asked Annie about it, then came and asked me about it. Later, there was a breach of our systems that had come from the hospital. Now she was missing, and the hovercraft that her parents owned was gone as well.

This didn't sound good.

Already dreading the answer, I turned to Annie. "What is the range on her parents' hovercraft?"

She looked at me and I could see the worry in her

eyes, as well. "Far," she said. "They bought the best one on the market right before the war, so it's supposed to be able to go a sizable distance without recharging, as well as being pretty fast - for a personal craft."

"Skrell," I cursed. My brother looked at me. "You're going to need to go with someone else on patrol," I told him. "Annie and I need to talk to the general."

"Okay, what am I missing?" he asked.

"She has a top-of-the-line hovercraft with a long range of travel. She's interested in finding out the intelligence level of the Puppet Master. She's been asking a lot of questions and she's now missing," I explained.

His eyes lit up in understanding. "She's gone for the crater," he said matter-of-factly.

I nodded.

"Okay," he sighed. "Are you sure you don't want me with you?"

I shook my head. "If I'm wrong, I'll be back in just a few," I said. "If I'm right, I'll pick you up on the way."

"Okay, go."

I looked at Annie, who nodded at me, and we began making our way to the general.

"Do you really think she'd do something like this?" I asked, trying one more time to verify my ideas.

She nodded as she jogged next to me. I slowed down my pace for her, not realizing that I had been walking that fast. "Yeah, she's the type. Kind of like Tella, and me."

Fantastic.

Another human woman with far too much impulsiveness.

DAPHNE

"*Estimated arrival time: five minutes,*" the onboard computer announced in its impersonal disembodied voice. I stirred in my seat, feeling as if someone had nailed my spine to it, and groaned as I looked out the window. The scenery remained the same as the past half an hour, a deserted landscape with barely any distinguishable features except the remains of the alien vessel, *Aurora*. Not for the first time since leaving Nyheim, I suspected the hovercraft had been travelling in circles.

But that wasn't exactly a surprise, given that the onboard computer had been announcing an ETA of five minutes for the past two hours or so. "Crap," I muttered, sitting straight in the chair and hitting the dashboard controls a couple of times. I disengaged the autopilot feature and assumed control of the hovercraft. For good measure, I shut off the navigation system as well.

Even though my parents' hovercraft was top-of-the-line, it was an urban model. The navigation system had been designed for city travel, and now that I was roaming through the wilderness, it was throwing a fit.

I wasn't sure of the crater's exact location, but it couldn't be that far away. Judging from the reports I had managed to grab from the government server, it was one of the few landmarks in this part of the desert, so I was counting on that to help me find it.

It wasn't easy, of course. I spent the next three and a half hours flying around aimlessly, and it didn't help that I had barely gotten any sleep. Even though I had tried to get some shut-eye as the autopilot worked its magic during the night, sleeping in a hovercraft seat wasn't exactly an easy task. I was about to turn the autopilot back on when I noticed something on the horizon. Squinting, my fingers curled tight around the controls, I then let out a triumphant shout as I realized I was looking at the crater.

Pushing the hovercraft's engines to the limit, I sped up toward the edge and only then began my descent. It was a controlled landing, which was pretty much a miracle—when I was younger, I used to sneak out of my parents' house and steal their hovercraft for the night, only to be caught when they discovered the countless dents caused by my reckless flying.

Mom would be proud.

Except for the fact I was using her hovercraft to do something that was pretty much illegal.

Illegal-ish? Maybe just strongly discouraged.

I tried not to think of that: nobody would know about this little field trip of mine, after all. Unless I found something of interest...but by then, the government would be more interested in hiring me than punishing me. This was a win-win situation.

Or so I hoped.

"And here we are," I whispered to myself as I shut the engines down. Popping the door open, I jumped out of the hovercraft and stretched my back, groaning as I heard it crack. I walked carefully toward the edge of the crater and looked at it with fascination.

It wouldn't be easy to climb down, and I hoped the climbing gear I had brought would suffice. If what I'd picked up from Annie and those reports were correct, the crater might somehow offer an explanation for the vines.

Like it or not, there was no other option but to climb down and look around.

I felt slightly anxious, but that was only reasonable. I had spent most of my career holed up inside a lab, and field work wasn't exactly part of a neuroscientist's job description. But here I was, breaking the mold.

Returning to the hovercraft, I dug my bags from the back and laid them on the sand tidily. Then, grabbing whatever food I had managed to steal from mom's kitchen, I sat on the hood of the hovercraft and had an improvised breakfast. Rappelling down a crater while hungry didn't strike me as a good idea, after all.

The sun was still rising on the horizon, lazily making its ascent up the sky, and I enjoyed the way the weather was slowly warming up. It almost convinced me to sleep for a couple of hours more, but I knew that in just a couple of hours the pleasant warmth would give way to a terrible heat, so I got to work the moment I was done with breakfast.

I was down on my knees, sorting through my equipment, when I started hearing a low humming sound. Confused, I looked around to see where the noise was coming from. I didn't see anything, so I stood up and used my hand to shade my eyes from the sun. That was when I saw *them*.

In the distance, tiny black dots seemed to be growing larger against the backdrop of a blue sky, the sun gleaming on their metallic surfaces. Just one heartbeat later and the dots grew large enough for me to realize I was looking at a small group of shuttles.

I froze then, not sure on what I should do.

Could those be government aircraft? Or were they just part of some commercial convoy making its way between cities?

I had absolutely no idea and, worst of all, there was no way for me to find out. If those were government shuttles, I was pretty screwed.

"Crap, crap, crap," I repeated over and over again, trying to come up with a solution. "Alright, calm down, Daphne," I finally chided myself, taking a deep breath as I closed my eyes. If the government wasn't coming after me, then I was worrying needlessly.

But if I was going to be detained, then it was already too late to do anything about it. I could only try to make the most out of the situation, which meant I had to work *fast*.

Replacing panic with determination, I ran toward the bags and grabbed some of the handheld equipment. I wasn't sure which equipment I would need, so I just decided to go for the ones I could carry. I glanced at the shuttles one more time and, realizing that they were drawing close, I started running away from the hovercraft.

There were a couple of dunes just a hundred feet or so away from where I had landed, and those would be the perfect cover. If I were lucky, the shuttles would ignore my hovercraft...if not, maybe I could sneak around my wannabe captors and try to collect some samples before my inevitable capture.

"Oh, shit!" I cried out as I got to the crest of one of the dunes, realizing that it dipped down toward another crater, one that was much smaller than the main one, probably no more than ten feet across. As the sand shifted under my feet, I tumbled forward and rolled down the dune fast, the world around me spinning wildly.

The world went dark when I dove straight into the smaller crater, and for a moment I was certain I was going to die.

I didn't.

I crashed through a lattice of something, too fast and too dark to make out what had saved me.

I landed at the bottom of the crater with a thud, feeling slightly dizzy but otherwise okay. I sat up, patted my body and breathed out with relief. No broken bones, so there was that.

Overhead, I could still hear the furious growl of engines, and I was pretty certain that the shuttles were already landing. I wanted to grab a few samples before I was caught, but it seemed that I wouldn't have the chance to do so...not if I were trapped in a dark hole in the ground, that was.

I was about to give up and call for help when I felt something brush against my leg. I stifled a scream and, fighting back panic, reached inside my bag and grabbed a flashlight. When I turned it on, I was surprised to see that there was a small vine sprouting from the ground, its tip gently nudging my ankle.

Well, that was unusual.

Which was exactly what I was here for.

"Hello, there," I whispered, grabbing a pair of shears to collect a sample. Normal procedure...except I wasn't expecting what happened next. As I spoke, the vine moved slightly, almost as if it were reacting to my voice.

It was *listening* to me.

TAKAR

"Skrell," the general said as Annie and I explained our hypothesis.

If he was as frustrated as I was by the situation, he at least kept his temper.

He looked at the both of us, staring at Annie hard, almost as if she were to blame for Daphne's probable behavior. Which was possible, but honestly, from the small time I'd spent with Daphne, I wasn't sure if anything would have held her back.

"Fine," he said as he turned his attention to me. "Gather a small team and go get her."

"And if she's discovered the creature and angered it?" I asked.

He gave a bit of side-nod. "Fine, make sure the team

is large enough to deal with trouble, but not too large. We still have too many issues here."

"Sir," I said with a quick salute. We exited his office before I turned to Annie. "Sorry, but you're not going."

"What? She's my friend," she argued.

I put my hands on her shoulders and held her still. "I understand that, but if things get bad, I'm going to need the team concentrating on stopping the creature, not protecting you. Besides, Karzin would never forgive me if anything happened to you."

With that, I walked away, getting on the comm and calling for Rokul, Sylor, and several of the combined city guard to meet me at the airfield in full combat gear.

No one argued or questioned, they simply acknowledged and met me there. I quickly explained the situation and told them what my plan was. I had already gotten the tracking information for the hovercraft, so I knew where she was heading. We would take a transport and chase her down, but if she arrived at the crater and somehow came into contact with the Puppet Master before we arrived, things could go bad.

Very bad.

Very quickly.

"One small problem," one of the human guards, Trevor, said. "The only transports we have available at the moment are the small ones."

"What? Why?" I demanded.

"Maneuvers and food deliveries," he answered.

"Fine," I growled. "Load up."

They were cramped, but workable, with enough room for four people. Rokul piloted one, Sylor piloted another, I piloted the last, making sure we were leaving space for Daphne.

If we found her.

We lifted off and I took the lead.

I brought up the tracking system, punched in the hovercraft's information, and turned my little ship in the right direction. We were flying towards the *Aurora's* home in the desert and the original hole the Puppet Master had created. After nearly two hours of flight, we arrived in the desert.

"Keep an eye out for anything that may indicate where she is, just in case she left the hovercraft," I ordered.

It wasn't long before I saw the hovercraft. I pushed my…we had to come up with a better name for these things…ship ahead. I saw a small shape standing outside the craft that turned and started running.

She was a persistent one, I had to admit. She had to know that she was in trouble, yet she wasn't going to give up. If she wasn't an annoyance to my life, I'd be impressed with her. She didn't seem the type to dive headfirst into danger. She seemed far too perky and far too ready with a smile to be the type willing to go on an adventure.

She disappeared behind a small dune as I landed. I shut down, unbuckled, grabbed my gear, and chased after her. The others were landing as I reached the dune she had jumped behind. I didn't find footprints as I had expected. Instead, I found another crater, this one nowhere near as large as the original.

This one was only ten feet across, if that.

"Did you get her?" I heard from behind me. Rokul and the others were approaching, weapons at the ready.

Daphne might not be a danger, but we'd all seen what the Puppet Master could do.

I shook my head.

"Then, did she go down the hole?" Trevor asked.

It was the only possible solution to her location. "Spread out, search the area. Just in case," I ordered. If she had found a way to get away without going down into the crater, we needed to figure that out first.

We searched the surrounding area, but found nothing. Not even her footprints.

She really had gone into the hole.

Skrell and double skrell.

I liked Annie, mostly. For a human, she didn't make me too annoyed. I was grateful to her for how she had fixed Karzin and made him happy, but her recklessness was not something to be admired, or emulated.

"What do we do?" my brother asked, snapping me out of my thoughts.

I groaned as the only option was to go down into the hole after her. "I'll go down," I said. "She's spoken to me, so she'll recognize my face and not be too scared by it."

"Are you sure? You're an ugly one," my brother teased. The others laughed as I glared at him.

"Back on point," I said. "I'll go down and bring her back. All of you stay up here."

"Why do we stay up here?" Trevor, one of the human guards who'd accompanied us, asked.

Sylor, who had been getting climbing gear prepared, answered. "If there's anything that goes wrong down there, it's better to only lose one member of the team instead of all of us."

"Exactly," I agreed. "Besides, if the Puppet Master attacks me down there, it would be nearly impossible for all of us to fight without hitting ourselves."

"Ah," Trevor said with a big nod. "Makes sense."

"Good, now help me secure the rigging so we don't lose him," Sylor ordered. While my brother helped me attach the climbing gear to myself, Sylor and Trevor found a place to anchor my guideline. The other two guards kept a lookout at the surrounding desert in case any vines or animals decided to attack.

"You sure about this?" Rokul asked me.

"No," I answered simply.

I didn't want to do this. I didn't want to chase after some idiot human with no concept of safety and no feelings towards anyone else's well-being. I was not happy with this woman.

"Just, be careful, okay," he said. "Remember what we saw on the trip into the first crater?"

I nodded.

It was more a case of what we didn't see.

And that was concerning.

Karzin's first encounter with the vines hadn't gone well. They attacked him relentlessly, viciously. There was speculation, from all of us, that Karzin's first encounter wasn't really his first one. The Puppet Master had been known to secrete a memory-loss gas when it attacked.

So we had no way of knowing.

"I believe that I'm ready," I said as we finalized the last buckle.

I took out a glow stick, snapped it to activate it, and then I slowly lowered myself down into the crater. I was unable to see the bottom of the hole, so I had no idea how far down it went.

Approximately ten to fifteen feet down, where the natural light started to disappear, I found a small ledge that was connected to a tunnel. I stopped my descent. I grabbed my glow stick and held it out into the tunnel. It looked to be a bit shorter than I was. If I traversed down the tunnel, I would have to do so at a slight stoop.

It was wide, however. My brother and I could have walked shoulder to shoulder and still not touch the sides.

At the end of the tunnel, I could see Daphne. I climbed onto the ledge and began to make my way towards her. She was covered in dirt, yet she was smiling.

It lit up her face, something I could see even from here.

What was she doing? I asked myself as I crawled towards her. Then I finally got a clear look. She was touching a vine. She was actually touching the vine, something we had warned the citizens of the city against.

Yet, here she was, touching it…wait…she was *petting* it. She was stroking it as though it were some sort of animal. How could she do that? Didn't she know it was dangerous? Was the vine making her forget?

Was that why she was touching it? She had forgotten it was dangerous?

I fumbled with my buckles, trying to unclip myself. I cursed Rokul and his inability to tie a proper knot or to properly clip me in. It took too many moments for me to finally unhook myself. As soon as I did, I got to my feet and rushed for Daphne.

She looked over at me and for the briefest of moments, I thought she didn't recognize me. Her mannerisms suggested that she didn't know who I was, then suddenly her eyes went wide.

"What are you doing here?" she asked.

I grabbed her and yanked her away from the vine. "Don't touch that thing. What is wrong with you?" I hadn't noticed how loud my voice was, but the tunnel around me began to shake.

She tried to pull away from me. "What are you doing?" she repeated angrily. "It wasn't doing anything to me."

"Enough!" I yelled.

I shouldn't have done that. The tunnel trembled and shook even more, sending dirt and debris falling. There was a rumbling sound as the shaking continued, eventually culminating in a loud crash as the opening to the tunnel collapsed. The roof of the tunnel continued to fall down the length of it, finally stopping maybe six feet away from us.

"Oh, no," Daphne whispered.

We were trapped, stuck underground with no way out, and a vine sitting right next to us.

And the day had started so well.

DAPHNE

Just as quickly as it had appeared, the vine slithered back into the ground. And all because of this stupid Skotan.

Had I thought he was hot?

All of that burned away in my irritation.

Pointing my flashlight at the ground, I tried to see where the vine had gone to but, of course, I couldn't find any sign of it anywhere. The cave-in and the screams from the Skotan had scared it, it seemed.

"You idiot," I hissed. "Look at what you've done."

"And what exactly have I done?" he asked me, arms folded over his chest as he stared at me. He didn't look too happy to be trapped in this tunnel with me, but I didn't care about his feelings. This was his fault. He didn't see it that way, though. "This is *your* fault, miss."

"Oh, really?" I threw back at him, feeling angrier by the second. "You were the one that came here screaming like a maniac. If you hadn't, we wouldn't be trapped in here."

"You were already trapped here, in case you hadn't noticed."

"No, I wasn't," I replied. "I fell here, sure, but the packed dirt of the crater side would be enough for me to climb back up."

"That doesn't sound like much of a plan," he sighed, shaking his head as if he were scolding a child.

God, why was he being so damn condescending? I knew I wasn't supposed to be here, but that didn't change the fact that this idiot's sudden appearance had made things a hundred times worse.

Especially because I knew I was on to something...the vines didn't seem as menacing as everyone believed, and I was pretty sure there was an intelligent being at play here.

I thought idly back to how he had felt when he had pulled me back and sheltered me from the cave in.

How his strong muscles had wrapped me against him.

With a deep breath, I willed myself to focus. Not hot, not hot.

"My plan was good enough."

"Really?" he insisted, cocking an eyebrow up. "I didn't know you had a grand plan. Care to share?"

I paused for a moment, not sure on what I should tell him. In the end, I just shrugged. "I'm pretty good at making plans up on the fly."

He just stared at me as if I had said the most idiotic thing in the universe, but I didn't pay him any attention. Turning my back to him, I placed my bag on the ground and started pulling my equipment out. I had fallen on top of the bag over and over again as I tumbled down the crater, and I needed to check if the equipment was still operational.

Even though I was pissed at him for causing the cave-in, I couldn't deny that this was the opportunity I needed. If we weren't trapped in here, I would already be on my way back to Nyheim. Now, though, I had the chance I needed to investigate.

"What are you doing?" he asked me, standing right behind me as he glanced at my equipment. "We don't have any time to play around. We have to return to the surface. We should start removing the blockage and—"

"No," I shook my head, a small grin spreading across my lips. "If you do that, you risk making things worse. You start removing the blockage, and there's going to be a further cave-in." He frowned then, but I could see he agreed with me. He still eyed the blockage for a couple of seconds, as if trying to confirm what I had told him, but his stern expression told me he had no choice but to agree with me.

Satisfied to see all of my equipment still worked, I started packing it all inside my bag once more. "We're trapped in here for the time being," I continued, looking back at him over my shoulder, "so we might as well use the opportunity to find something worth examining."

"You're insane," he sighed. "We're trapped in here, and your main concern is collecting samples? Do you even know what these vines are capable of? We're in danger here."

"Are we?" I snapped. "Because I didn't feel like I was in any danger...before you showed up and started making a scene, that is. Besides, we have no choice but go deeper down the tunnel. Unless, of course, you have a better idea."

He didn't bother with a reply. Instead, he grabbed the radio hanging from his belt and brought it up to his face. "This is Takar," he started, holding one of the buttons on his radio. "I've located the human female, but there has been a cave-in. We're going to try and find an alternate way out."

There were a few seconds of silence, the static noise coming from the radio bouncing against the tunnel walls, but then there was a crackle and a voice. "*Copy that*," the voice replied, sounding calm and collected.

"We're going to start looking for other craters that might serve as an exit point. We'll also start doing sonic scans to see if we can map out the tunnels."

"Copy that," Takar sighed, and then continued saying something else. I was no longer paying attention, though. I started advancing through the tunnel, using my flashlight to light the way, and kept my eyes peeled to see if I could find any more vines.

"Hey," Takar cried out, his heavy footsteps echoing through the tunnel as he made his way toward me. "We should stick together. Don't rush ahead without me."

"Then keep up," I grinned.

"Do you even have any idea what you're doing?" he insisted. "You don't know what you're dealing with here, miss."

"The name's Daphne," I frowned, stopping for a moment to look at him. "And, yes, I know exactly what I'm doing here. I'm conducting an investigation into the Puppet Master. I think it's time someone does it, don't you?"

"What do you think the general has been trying to do?" he threw back at me. "We have a whole team of scientists working day and night to—"

"Well, it's not working, is it?" I cut him short, now carefully analyzing the walls with my flashlight, hoping to see any vestige of the vines. "The way I see it, the government is more preoccupied with trying to prevent further incidents than trying to get to the bottom of this."

"Of course we're worried about further incidents!"

"Yeah," I nodded, "but it's not like you'll be able to do it while having no idea what you're dealing with. I mean, you call it the Puppet Master...but do you even have any idea what it is?"

"A dangerous threat," he replied almost immediately, almost as if he didn't care about a further explanation. Why did these soldiers only see the world in black and white? Either things were dangerous, or they were inoffensive...for them, there was no middle ground, apparently.

"Are you even sure it's a creature?"

"Might not be," he shrugged. "But it's dangerous all the same."

"See? That's the problem with you guys," I shook my head. "If you really want to stop things from getting any crazier, you have to *understand* what you're dealing with. And that requires a thorough examination."

"And do you think you're the person to do it?"

"Actually," I smiled, "I do."

TAKAR

Getting back to the surface anytime soon was out of the question.

Getting this woman to believe that I was right about the Puppet Master was out of the question.

Getting myself to calm down and fully understand this insane woman was out of the question.

Unfortunately, those were the only questions I had and I needed to have them answered.

Daphne was, by far, the most annoyingly persistent —or persistently annoying—woman of any species that I had ever met. She was insistent on following through with her 'study' of the Puppet Master. She refused to give in.

"Why won't you simply accept the fact that what you're doing is wrong?" I asked her.

"How am I wrong?" she asked. "Wait, why are we about to have the same argument we just had?" She turned away from me and started studying the tunnel walls as we walked. She was enthralled by what she was seeing.

I saw...dirt.

"What do you mean 'have the same argument'?" I asked, walking behind her. "I didn't realize we were finished."

She waved me off as though I were a minor irritant not worth the effort. She continued walking, studying, and talking to herself about what she saw. She was... infuriating, yet impressive.

If she had been a Skotan, this stubbornness would have been relished. A flare of interest went up my spine as I realized that even the lack of scales didn't deter me.

Skrell. I must be borderline intoxicated by this human woman.

We continued walking in silence for approximately twenty minutes, stopping often so she could look at the walls for one reason or another.

The tunnel sloped down, at a gentle, but noticeable, angle. Not ideal. Not at all. But maybe ahead we'd come to an opening. Some sort of branching, and could work our way back up towards the surface.

Deciding to try a different tactic, I decided to ask her a simple question. "Are you a geologist like Annie?"

"No, not a geologist, and definitely not like Annie," she answered over her shoulder.

"Then, if you don't mind my asking, why are you studying the walls so much?"

She stopped walking and turned to look back at me. "What? Just because I'm not a geologist, I'm not allowed to study things like dirt and soil? Who said that I was only allowed to do one thing?" I think I had irritated her. "Do you big-ass aliens only do one thing?"

"Well, no," I answered. Before I could explain that we were a very adaptive crew, she flew into even more of an outrageous defense of herself.

"Oh, so you people are allowed to be multitalented, but we measly humans have to be limited to a single interest, huh?" she put her hands on her hips as she spoke. "Too bad the multiple talent gene didn't make it to you."

"And what is that supposed to mean?" I asked.

She snorted in laughter. "Of course you don't know. Yesterday? Your little desk job thing you were on? You suck at it." She grinned as she turned away from me and started walking again.

"I never once said that I enjoyed speaking to people like you," I shot back as I too, began walking. "I would much rather be doing something productive than sitting at a desk."

"Then we actually have something in common

then," she shot back. She reached out and touched part of the wall.

"Will you stop doing that?" I demanded.

"What?"

"Stop touching things," I answered. "The Puppet Master is dangerous and can emit some sort of gas that causes short-term memory loss."

"Really?" she asked. It sort of sounded as though she were being sarcastic, but there was a hint of actual curiosity and fear mixed into her voice. Then it was gone. "Well then, tell me something, Mister Big and Red, if it can make us forget, why hasn't it done that yet?"

I…I actually had no answer.

"Thought so," she said triumphantly. "Now, if this thing was so dangerous, why didn't it completely destroy any of the cities? Why didn't it crush Nyheim, instead of just contain us? Why did it let me touch it?"

Again, I had no answer.

"Uh-huh," she said with an overexaggerated nod. "You don't know any more about this thing than I do, do you? Do you?" At my hesitation, she continued. "I didn't think so. That's why I'm down here. I'm trying to learn about this, get some *real* information about it."

"*'Real'* information?" I sputtered. "Very well, here's some real information. It can emit a memory-loss gas. It controls anything and everything that is plant-like, including the semi-sentient ones. It can encompass entire cities in vines that are thicker than both of us combined. Based on what you and I have already seen, it has tunnels all throughout this area. The information that Leena and Tella have already gleaned from the vines show that it has an incredible rate of healing far beyond anything we understand."

She pursed her lips together and gave me a drawn-out "Ooh. So you have learned a couple things. It's dangerous, but not outrightly so. It's mobile, or so you think. It's controlling, but we don't know how. And, if it can heal so damn fast, why did it let you take down the dome?"

I opened my mouth to respond, then shut it in confusion. I was grateful she was still walking ahead of me and not looking back to see me like this.

I hadn't thought of that last point in the same way. Could the Puppet Master have *allowed* us to escape?

"See? You got nothing," she went on. "That's why we need something more in-depth, more complete to look into. If we want to know what this thing is, we need to get closer and figure it out."

"You're just using that as an excuse for your own curiosity," I shot back.

She shrugged. "And?" She stopped and looked back at me. "So what if I am? If I satisfy my curiosity, isn't that better for all of us?"

It made sense. Skrell, but it made sense. However...

"Do you even know what you're looking for, or are you making that up as you go, as well?" I asked, partially making fun of her lack of planning and her penchant for not thinking things through.

She had no answer. At last, I finally had something that prevented her from talking!

She spun back around and resumed walking through the tunnel. She no longer stopped to examine the walls, she just walked at a fairly brisk pace. I truly believe that I had touched a nerve with her.

I was about to say something to her when, suddenly, the tunnel ended.

But instead of a blank dirt wall, or another cave-in, we looked out onto an underground paradise.

Stretched out for a distance well beyond one of Nyheim's city blocks was a cavern. The small pathway that we had been walking on sloped gently down into a cavern filled with small land bridges, columns of stalagmites and stalactites that stretch dozens, if not hundreds, of feet up and down, some of them connecting to create giant pillars.

There were thin streams webbing their way across the floor of the cavern, some ending in small pools of water, others disappearing into the walls on the far side. Plants of shapes, sizes, and colors that I didn't know could possibly exist filled the cavern, lighting it with some form of bioluminescence.

"Oh," was all that Daphne said, her voice full of wonder.

I was not inclined to add much to her statement. I was captivated by the intense beauty of what I was looking at. I looked up, towards the top of the cavern, and I could see roots protruding from the ceiling, roots that must have belonged to something, though I wasn't quite sure what, since we were underneath a desert.

But I didn't care about the oddity of a thick root system underneath a barren desert. This place was far too beautiful and amazing for me to concern myself with something that could potentially be explained as an ancient root system of plants from long ago that are in a hibernation state until the climate above returns to a conducive environment for them to grow again.

None of that mattered to me as I stared down at the magnificence of the cavern again. Blues and reds and oranges and yellows stood out against the greens and purples and...I didn't even recognize those colors. The combinations of colors that I never had believed could go together in harmony filled this place with a beauty indescribable.

At the bottom of the cavern, I could see a giant, bulbous plant that carried green and blue coloring open to reveal a white center. It must have stood easily twice my height for it to look as large as it did from up here. I had never wished to know more about the anatomy of plant life than in that moment. It felt inadequate to merely call it a bulbous plant with a center.

The green and blue coloring of the bulb was replaced with yellow and red on the inside of the petals. The white…center…almost seemed to pulsate for a few moments before the flower closed again. Its closing almost felt sad.

Daphne, without thinking, I was sure, reached out and touched my arm. She was just as enthralled, maybe even more so, with what we were seeing. "Look," she said breathlessly. She was pointing at a section of the cavern that seemed to be moving. They were vines, and they were thicker than the trees up top, some even thicker than the ones used to encase the city.

They were horizontal, most of them, and seemed to create a dam for what looked to be a large lake. I wasn't sure if it was water or not, but the rippling surface looked like water from here. Some of the vines, at the ends of the 'dam' turned and became vertical, stretching up to the ceiling.

It was more than my imagination could have come up with.

And all of it belonged to the Puppet Master. It had to. I had no other explanation for it. Whatever this creature was, it was responsible for so much more than just simple vines.

I looked down at Daphne to see that she was in as much, if not more, awe than I was.

I don't believe she even noticed that she still held onto my arm.

And I… I didn't mind it a bit.

DAPHNE

If Takar said something to me, I didn't hear him. Hell, he could throw a bucket of ice water over my face and I wouldn't have noticed.

The cavern opened up to a chamber large enough to fit several towering buildings. Even with the naturally formed pillars and columns, I had a hard time believing that this cavern had stood the test of time without caving in.

Now I had just about a whole world to explore down here.

"We could use that sturdy one there," Takar's voice pushed its way into the peripherals of my hearing.

"What are you talking about?" I asked, only half paying attention to the words my mouth formed.

"The pillar there. I just said that. Weren't you listening?" I heard the annoyance in his voice.

"No," I smirked.

"I'm guessing that's a theme with you?" Takar replied coolly.

"We'll have to see," I shrugged. I wasn't used to working directly with another person. Collaborations were commonplace at the hospital, but it was more of an "I do my job and hand it off to the next person" kind of situation. It was different in surgery, but it'd been a while since someone went under in my surgical suite.

"Now, what are you talking about?" I dramatically rolled my neck to look at him.

"That pillar there," he pointed to an impressive rock formation. "I've got grappling hooks. Only one set, so you'll have to hold on to me. If we can get to the top, I'm willing to bet the surface layer is thin enough for me to break through."

"Sounds reasonable," I admitted. Thinking Takar's explanation was finished, I turned my attention back to a particularly beautiful bloom to my right. I felt sure it hadn't been there a moment ago, though I was distracted by the pretty picture laid out before me. I ran a finger along a lovely deep blue petal when I heard Takar clear his throat.

"What?" I asked.

"Let's go," he gestured impatiently.

"Oh, you meant now?" I furrowed my brow. "Are you in a hurry? What's the harm in taking half an hour or so to learn about this place? Who knows? Maybe one of these flowers will unlock the mystery that is the Puppet Master."

"I have orders to-"

Sensing the refusal before he could get it out of his mouth, I whirled around and snatched the comm unit from his utility belt. I suspected getting the drop on Takar was a difficult job, but he never expected me to make a move like that.

"Hey!" he growled. I skittered out of reach while I brought up the last unit he had contact with. Or at least I thought I did. The display was in his own language, but the design wasn't very different from the ones we had.

"Takar, what's your status?" A voice just as gruff as Takar's came through.

"This is actually the young lass you were sent to rescue," I twirled away from Takar and took a few steps down one of the naturally formed ramps in the cavern wall. "I'm trying to prove a point. I've found something amazing down here and I wish to study it. Are you all right with waiting a little while longer so that I can gather information?"

I flashed a grin at Takar that I knew would make his blood boil. He glared at me, arms crossed over his broad chest. Apparently, he'd given up trying to get his unit back. All the better.

Laughter came through the connection.

"That's fine by us," one of Takar's teammates chuckled.

"Thank you," I trilled before disconnecting. I tossed the comm unit back to Takar. "See? I told you there's no harm in taking a moment to learn something new."

The more he glared at me the wider my smile grew.

"Come on!" I dared him. "You can't possibly be this boring all the time."

"I'm not boring," Takar muttered. If I didn't know better, I'd say he was getting defensive.

"Prove it," I challenged.

"I rescued you, what more proof do you need?" I hadn't expected him to take the bait. Now that he had, I was finally having a little fun.

"Being a hero doesn't prove anything. You can be a hero and still be boring. And, if I'm remembering correctly, your little rescue caused the cave-in that forced us to come this way," I replied. Takar was seething. I held back a giggle.

"If you hadn't blindly jumped down a hole this wouldn't have happened," he replied.

"It's a good thing I did, then!" I beamed. "Want to really prove that you're not boring?"

"How?" he muttered begrudgingly.

"Hold this." I shoved a piece of equipment into his hands. I wouldn't need it. I dug through my bag, looking for one particular device. As I did, I continued to pass things for Takar to hold.

"Ah! There we go." I pulled the device I was looking for out of my bag. Naturally, it had fallen to the very bottom. The bag was practically empty now. I looked over at Takar. Even with hands so large, he was struggling to hold everything.

"You all right?" I asked, holding back a grin. Takar muttered something about being a trained soldier, not a lackey. I opened my bag so he could tip the unwanted devices back into it.

"Gently!" I warned him. "Each one of those costs more than you make in a year."

"You have no idea how much I make in a year," Takar replied.

"I don't have to. I know those things are worth more than both of our yearly wages combined," I said.

"Then why would you dump them all into an unprotected bag and jump into a crater with them?" Takar asked.

"Where's your sense of adventure? Doesn't the thrill of discovery excite you?" I asked, mostly teasing him at this point. Takar responded with a scowl. "You're pretty cute when you're grumpy."

"I'm not grumpy," Takar insisted in a very grumpy manner. This time, I didn't hold back my laughter.

"Come on, Mr. Grumpy."

I turned my back on him and carefully made my way down a jagged pathway leading down to the bottom of the cavern.

I examined the device in my hands. It was a scanner that gave rough estimates of brain activity. It was supposed to be used on, you know, a body part containing a brain. Based on my experience, plant vines didn't usually have brains.

Then again, this was a plant that broke every rule in the plant book. For all I knew, I was walking on its brain.

The brain scanner was roughly the size of my own hand. Even if something near me did have brain activity, my device would likely be too small to give me accurate results. On a whim, I lifted my device and scanned the portion of vine nearest to me. There was a minimal reading, which wasn't surprising. All living things gave off some sort of reading.

"I'll figure out what you really are," I murmured to the vine as if it could hear me. "There's got to be more to you than everyone thinks."

I suddenly became aware that Takar wasn't behind me. I looked over my shoulder. He was at the base of the natural decline, running his fingers along one of the rocky pillars.

"Find something?" I called to him.

"Not sure," he called back, his brow furrowed. When he wasn't focused on scowling at me, he was quite handsome.

Pity that didn't happen more often.

When he didn't elaborate, I rolled my eyes and tucked my scanner back into my bag.

"Is this some kind of guessing game?" I asked him.

"What are you talking about?" Takar replied.

"Do I have to guess what you found or are you going to tell me?" I prompted.

"These pillars weren't made naturally," Takar replied. "I suspect those ramps aren't either."

"They look naturally made to me," I replied, though I wasn't an expert by any means.

"It's subtle," Takar informed me. "These were formed by something huge, but not terribly powerful. I'd even call this a delicate job. Judging by the placement, I'd also call it deliberate."

"But why?" I asked.

"I couldn't tell you," Takar replied. "It certainly wasn't made by humans. Your terraforming technology isn't this advanced."

"I wasn't aware we even had terraforming technology," I admitted.

"Not surprising." I caught the smirk in the corner of Takar's mouth.

"Don't be a dick," I chuckled. "Could this be Xathi tech?"

"If it is, I haven't seen anything like it before," Takar replied. "But I don't think it's Xathi. The terraforming was done over time."

"You can tell that?" I asked.

"Can't you?" Another smirk. Now it was my turn to scowl. "That's a fair question since you make a living looking at tiny changes in the brain."

"Yes. The brain. Not earth. Not rock. Brain. Squishy, pink, human brains," I replied.

"Human brains are pink?" Takar asked.

"Yes," I replied. "Isn't yours?"

"I don't think so," Takar replied.

"Don't you know?" I mimicked his mocking tone.

"Very funny," Takar scoffed. I stuck my tongue out at him.

"Well, while you're solving the terraforming mystery, I'm going to keep looking around."

Leaving Takar to stare at rocks, I made my way over to a few vines with luscious, bright blooms.

"How do you grow such beautiful flowers?" I wondered aloud.

"Are you talking to a plant?" Takar called to me.

"Yes," I responded. "Don't eavesdrop. It's rude."

"It has to be a two-way conversation before it's considered eavesdropping," he sighed.

Annoying him was fun.

Not nearly as fun as examining the vines one by one. I figured the thickest vine would yield the most results, though I wasn't sure what I needed to look for. I decided to use all of my handheld devices, just to see what I could dig up.

And if it annoyed Mr. Grumpy a little more?

That was alright, too.

TAKAR

I was still concerned over what had affected the rock formations, shaped them into these forms.

Annie had talked to me once, while she was waiting for Karzin to finish his reports. It had been interesting enough that I'd spent a little time reading up on the field.

Not a lot. Just enough to make sure I could better follow what she was talking about next time.

Now that she and Karzin were mated, there would be a next time to talk.

This didn't seem like it would be formed by flowing water. The shapes were smooth, but this was different from what I'd seen on the tablet.

The only thing that made sense to me was the Puppet Master and its vines. I knew what the vines felt like, rough, almost scaly. If they'd been drawn back and forth through the stone, wrapping around for some reason, that might cause these strange formations.

Another option, based on our excursions upon this planet thus far, was whatever race had left behind the ruins and the rift device could have made these, as well. I took out one of my scanners and began scanning and taking pictures. "Rokul?" I called for my brother over the comm.

"I'm still here," he answered. He was having far too much fun with this.

With a shake of my head, I got back on the comm. "I'm sending you some pictures and video of what we're looking at down here. Send it back, tagged for Amira and her team. Make sure you save a copy this time."

"Wow," he came back. "One time I forget to save a video and I never hear the end of it." His voice was filled with fake indignation as he kept talking. "Why can't you just forgive me, brother? Why?"

I turned off the comm. I wasn't in the mood for his humor at the moment. I did as I said I was going to do. I took pictures of the striations on the rocks, the way the formations looked, and then pictures and video of the cavern itself. It made me uneasy, but still filled me with wonder to look at it, to see how life had somehow found a way to establish itself and thrive underground.

Even if that life was due to the Puppet Master, it was a magnificent sight.

I risked turning the comm on again to ensure that my brother had gotten the images and saved them.

He was still talking, "…believe that you're not even answering me. You're purposefully ignoring your older brother and letting him just flutter in the winds of abandonment." I could hear the laughter in the background and I could imagine my brother overdoing it, making this entire diatribe of his into an overdramatic production.

I sighed, then whispered, just to make him pay attention. "Are you finished yet?"

"One more, then I'm done," came his answer. "Ahem…why can't you just let your dear old brother live the life he wants to live? Just forgive me already."

I waited.

"Okay," his voice as calm as it could be. "I'm done." The laughter in the background was still audible.

I…while I was buried underground with an impossibly irritating beautiful woman and possibly the biggest threat we've faced, at least on a planetary level, my brother was joking around and acting like a fool.

No wonder I had always been forced to be the responsible one. "Did you receive the pictures and video I sent?" I asked.

"Got them. Sent them. And," he said quickly, "I have them saved. I even made duplicate files just in case."

"Thank you," I said. I hoped he could hear the feeling of annoyance in my voice.

"In all seriousness, though," he came back on. "How are you doing down there?"

"As best as can be expected, I guess," I answered. As I talked to him, I spotted Daphne, rubbing and caressing one of the vines while she had her small scanner out. "I'll get back to you. I have to deal with this ketonsin woman."

"Have fun," his voice came back before I turned off the comm.

"What are you doing?" I asked Daphne as I approached her. The look on her face was pure wonder and amusement. I was forced to admit that she looked to be in her element down here. I don't remember any of the other women looking so happy and content when they were working or studying something. It was an attractive look on her.

She looked at me and told me to hush. While it wasn't unexpected of her to treat me that way, it still rankled.

"Can you please not touch the vine that way?" I asked, a bit quieter.

"Why not?" she asked, her voice matching mine,

calmer now, soothing. Maybe this place wasn't so bad after all.

If it could pacify her and not make her so much of a pain in my backside, maybe I could leave her down here?

No, I couldn't leave her.

And really, I didn't want to.

"Because it's dangerous," I answered. "How many times do I need to say it?"

"I guess until you say it right," she responded. "It's not 'dangerous,' per se, it merely has the capability to be dangerous…sort of like you," she added.

"What's that supposed to mean?" I demanded.

She shrugged as she continued looking at her scanner and touching the vine. "Think it through, big guy. You're dangerous, but not inherently so. You don't just go around breaking and shooting everything, do you?"

"No, I don't," I answered. "I'm much more aware of my actions and surroundings than that."

"Well," she said. "I suspect the Puppet Master is the same way."

"How do you figure?" I asked.

"Has it destroyed an entire city or settlement yet? Has it killed everyone it could?" she asked.

"No, not exactly," I answered. "But it did kill some people and destroy some buildings," I told her.

She looked at me. "I've been thinking about that," she said. "Did it actually kill those people, or did they die because of what happened?"

"What's the difference?"

She flashed me a *you're stupid* look, then took a deep breath and let it out slowly. "Did the Puppet Master's vines specifically kill anyone?"

"Well, no, not exactly, but..." I answered.

"Well," she interrupted, "then they died as a result of the PM's actions. Which means that it may not have exactly meant to kill those people, it just happened."

"Doesn't mean that it's innocent," I countered.

"Never said it was," she said with a shrug. "Those people dying because of what the PM did is terrible, but I'm trying to say that it might not have killed them on purpose. Just like it didn't destroy the city, it wasn't trying to cause permanent damage. Which means that it's not inherently dangerous."

I thought about what she had explained, and as much as I didn't want to, it made a weird sort of sense. It didn't absolve the Puppet Master from what it had done, but it did shine a different light on it, if she was right.

She was back to touching the vine, but this time I noticed the vine doing something different. It was pulsating, in a way...almost as if it were...breathing? It seemed normal that if it were merely a creature, it would need to breath, but this vine was as big as I was and the concept of it breathing …farfetched to me.

It bothered me, yet Daphne seemed perfectly content with what it was doing, as if breathing through a vine was perfectly normal.

"Come here," she whispered to me. I stepped closer and she reached out for my hand. "Feel this," she said as she tried to place my hand on the vine.

I snatched it away, not interested in that at all. "What are you trying to do?" I demanded.

She huffed. "I was just trying to let you feel the vine."

"I've touched it before," I said, referring back to the vines that had domed-in the city.

"Did you ever notice the heat radiating from it?" she asked, her voice filled with that amazing tone of hers that made me feel as if she thought I was the dumbest person around.

"Yes," I answered, letting my own tone of annoyance play through. "It was radiating the heat of the sun that it was blocking. What of it?"

"Well, if it was radiating the heat of the sun, then how do you explain that this vine is so warm?" she asked. "It's not on the surface."

That was certainly odd. I was at a loss.

"Do you know what that means?" she asked, obviously rhetorically because she didn't bother waiting for me to answer. "It means that this is not a simple plant. Plants that generate heat do so in tiny amounts, even here, where the plant life is admittedly stranger than usual. Only animals generate their own heat, just like we do."

"Now you're saying that the Puppet Master is not a sentient plant, but a sentient animal?" I asked, not bothering to hide my disbelief.

"Maybe not necessarily an animal, per se," she said, "But something we can't easily classify. Something more. Think about it. You and I generate our own body heat, and we're not plants. This thing is generating its own body heat, as well…" she trailed off.

"And you think that means that this thing is… what…an animal, or at least a not-entirely-plant-like creature?" I guessed.

"Precisely."

"And that's supposed to mean something important?" I asked, mostly out of aggravation. I knew that it did. Of course it would.

If she was correct in her assessment, that meant that we had been dealing with the Puppet Master incorrectly. If it was some sort of beast, then there was a slight chance that it was intelligent enough to understand its actions and it was merely defending itself.

And if it was some sort of sentient being, like Tella

had suggested once, and Daphne seemed to be hinting now, there might be a chance at communication.

"Well, yeah. We need to find the head, or whatever holds the brain. We need to see if we can communicate with it," she said, echoing my thoughts.

She was exuberant now with the idea that this may be more than a thinking plant.

"No," I immediately said. "We stay here, where there's a chance for us to get out by climbing the vines and cutting through to the surface. We can't risk going any deeper into whatever this is."

"You go, then," she said. "I'm going to go look." As she turned away from me, I reached out and gently, yet firmly, held her by the arm.

"No," I said, pulling her back towards me. As she protested, a small tendril-like vine came from under one of the other vines and wrapped around her other arm. There was a short moment of fighting with the vine, then I had enough.

I drew my blaster and shot the vine, watching in satisfaction as the tendril splintered and broke apart.

As I pulled Daphne behind me, she let out a muffled scream and yanked her arm from my grasp. I looked back to see hundreds of small vines wrapping themselves around her, forming an egg-like cocoon around her.

I heard her scream again.

I aimed my blaster, but didn't pull the trigger. There was too much of a chance that I would hit her, as well.

I holstered it, then reached out, grabbed the vines, and pulled. Despite my straining, nothing happened.

I pulled out my knife and started cutting at it, but for every vine I cut, another replaced it.

What was I supposed to do?

DAPHNE

I panicked the moment the vines enveloped me.

Which, I must say, was a perfectly reasonable reaction, if not entirely scientific of me.

They sprouted from the ground fast, and started wrapping themselves around me without giving me a chance to fight back. In just a few heartbeats, I was completely trapped inside a cocoon of sorts, the vines slithering together as they formed an almost impenetrable wall around me.

I could hear Takar shouting from the outside, but my heart was drumming so loudly I couldn't make out what he was saying. I started hyperventilating then, fear gripping me tight. All I could think about was that I had been so naive to think there'd be no danger to this...and now I would have to pay the price. I could already imagine the vines wrapping themselves around my neck, choking the life out of me, and I started thrashing inside the cocoon.

I couldn't die like this.

I simply couldn't.

Suddenly, though, the little green tendrils that were around my wrists and ankles slid back, and I slumped down inside the cocoon. The vines were no longer holding me, and there was at least a foot of space between me and the cocoon's inner wall.

I took a few deep breaths, trying to calm myself down, and closed my eyes for a second.

I could hear Takar moving outside, striking the cocoon over and over again with what I assumed to be a blade, and that just made the vines pack themselves even more tightly, strengthening the cocoon's outer shell.

Could they be reacting to what Takar was doing? Could it be that they were trying to protect me from him?

"Takar!" I shouted, suddenly realizing what was happening. It all made sense. "Stop it! Whatever it is you're doing, stop it right now!"

"What the hell are you talking about, woman?" he growled, his voice coming at me as if he were standing on the other side of the planet.

I kept on hearing his repeated blows against the cocoon, and so I just raised my voice again.

"Just stop it," I shouted, realizing that I wasn't in complete darkness. There were a few holes that allowed the light to filter through, and I looked for one large enough to allow me to peer outside. Pressing one eye against it, I saw Takar standing just a few feet away from the cocoon, looking completely furious. There was a knife in his left hand, and his right one was resting on the butt of his gun.

"Just stand still, Daphne," he continued, unholstering his gun and pointing it toward the cocoon. "I'm going to try and shoot it, but you have to tell me where to aim. I don't want to hit you."

"Are you even listening to me?" I cried out. "Put that gun away right now!"

"Are you insane? That thing is trying to kill you!"

"No, it's not," I tried to argue. "Please, Takar, I need you to trust me on this. Can you put your gun away and stand still?"

"Are you sure?" he asked me, shaking his head all the same. He probably thought I was acting like a complete nutjob, but I didn't care.

Takar would just make things worse if he kept on trying to stab or shoot the vines, and I wasn't about to let the situation spiral down into chaos.

"Please," I begged him, and this time he took a

couple of steps back and holstered his gun. I breathed out with relief the moment I saw him do it, and then ran my tongue over my parched lips. I wasn't entirely sure if what I was about to do would work, but something inside me told me I was on the right track.

"Takar doesn't mean to hurt you. *We* are not here to hurt you," I started saying in a low, soothing whisper, brushing my fingertips over the grooves on the cocoon's inner wall. I stroked the vines softly, almost as if I was petting a small creature, and I could almost feel them relax under my touch. "Takar isn't going to shoot. He's just worried about me. He means no harm."

I kept on speaking, reassuring the vines no harm would come to them or me, and I was pretty damn certain that they were listening.

I could feel them pulse under my fingertips, relaxing ever so slightly, and the more I spoke the more I started believing the vines weren't just listening...they actually understood what I was telling them.

After a while, the vines finally started loosening. The space I had inside the cocoon grew from one foot to two, and then three and four, and it wasn't long before the vines started retreating. I watched it happen, slack-jawed, mesmerized by their fluid and elegant moves as the cocoon opened.

"Daphne!" Takar cried out, immediately taking one step toward me. He grabbed me as I stumbled out of the cocoon, an expression of pure worry on his face. He eyed the vines for a moment, still not trusting them, but then turned his undivided attention back to me. "Are you okay?"

I said nothing, still trying to process what had happened. That just made Takar even more concerned, and he started patting my body down, looking for any wound or injury. I felt a shiver run up my spine as I felt the gentle touch of his fingertips on my skin, and my heart skipped a beat. I let him do it without saying a word, just enjoying his closeness, and he only pulled back when he realized I was looking at him.

"Daphne? Are you okay?" he asked once more, and this time I couldn't stop myself from smiling. I was no longer afraid, nervous, or anxious...I was completely ecstatic over what had just happened.

"I'm more than just okay!" I cried out, turning around to look at the vines once more. They were relaxed now, as if they were keeping an eye on us, intently listening to every word we said. "This is big, Takar! Don't you realize what just happened?"

"Not exactly," he admitted. "Other than you were buried in vines, and now you're not."

"The Puppet Master listened to me," I tried to explain. "Not only that, but it understood everything I was saying."

"And what were you saying?"

"I explained that we weren't a threat, and that we hadn't come here to cause it any harm," I continued. "And that's when the vines pulled back and freed me. This is real intelligence at work, I know it! We need to look into this!"

"I don't know if we—"

"Look," I cut him short. "We have a real opportunity here. The Puppet Master isn't being hostile toward us right now, but that may change if more people come crashing through the tunnels or if we try to force a way out. Let's not throw this opportunity away, alright? Your entire team of scientists hasn't had a breakthrough for who knows how long, but today we can make a difference. I just need you to trust me."

He frowned and, averting his gaze, exhaled sharply. I could almost see the gears inside his head turning, but I wasn't worried.

Takar seemed like the kind of soldier that prided himself on being a worthy asset, and he knew that his general was aching to find out more about the Puppet Master. Even though he had been dragged into this unwittingly, I was pretty sure he wouldn't pass on the opportunity.

"Fine," he relented, just like I had expected. "But I want you to be careful."

"I'm always careful," I laughed, reaching for him and grabbing his hand. Before he could protest, I started pulling him further into the caverns. The answer we needed to solve the Puppet Master riddle was somewhere in this cavern system, and I wasn't going to stop before figuring it out.

Come hell or high water.

Or Takar.

TAKAR

For one of the few times in my life, I wasn't in control of the situation, or even around someone in control that I trusted.

I was, instead of being in control, being dragged down a maze of tunnels by this woman who was no longer annoying, but was now…interesting.

Even if I did think she was trying to get us killed.

She had managed to find a way to endear herself to the Puppet Master, and that endearment had led to the Puppet Master putting a protective vine cocoon around her when it thought that I was threatening her.

Then, to add even more confusion to my life, she had gently caressed the vines of the cocoon and *talked* to them…and they listened.

She had done something that none of us had

attempted to do, and it worked. She had somehow managed to get whatever this creature was to listen, to treat her kindly, to protect her, and to convince it that I wasn't a danger to it. As if I could have caused it any real harm. If it was capable of surrounding an entire city with vines hundreds of feet in height, I sincerely doubted that I would be able to do more than cause it to itch.

I had allowed this woman to pull me along in her search for wherever the head, or brain, or control center, or whatever allowed the Puppet Master to think, was located, and I actually found myself enjoying it.

Not the being dragged part, but the investigation part. I honestly found myself looking forward to finding out what the Puppet Master was, and not even from a military standpoint.

I had grown up as a very inquisitive child, always more interested in researching something to discover what it was about while my brother had been the more outgoing type. We had stayed that way until a rogue tribe attacked our country, forcing me to abandon my life of study and take up a life of training.

This, however, was an opportunity to investigate a lifeform that no one knew anything about, and that appealed to me. It called to my more inquisitive nature. I knew that if I had not been forced into fighting, I would have pursued a more scientific line of the military life.

Granted, there was the chance for something terrible and deadly to happen, but since nothing had yet occurred, it was worth chancing the danger. To find out if this was a sentient being, if it was something that could hold a conversation and be reasoned with…I felt tingles throughout my body at the thought of it.

It was an interesting sensation to feel that tingle again.

I could almost hear Karzin and Rokul in my head, trying to call me out for this feeling. I didn't care. Sylor would have approved, at least on an intellectual, just-for-study level.

My brother would have made fun of me…not for being interested in investigating this, but for letting this small human woman drag me along. After all my grumbling about our team members falling to their mates...

I ducked my head to avoid hitting it on a low portion of whatever tunnel Daphne was pulling me down.

It wasn't that she was my mate. Of course not. I stopped again to accommodate another low-lying ceiling, it was just that by letting her pull me along, I had no other choice but to follow for her protection.

That was it. Keeping to the mission, keeping her safe.

"So, what's the plan?" I asked as we turned down yet another tunnel.

"Not a clue," she smiled over her shoulder. "I'm just kind of going until we find the head."

I took a grip of her hand and stopped, yanking her to a halt right along with me. "Hey," she cried out. "What was that for?"

"You really don't have a plan?" I asked.

She shrugged. "I sorta have one. I want to find the head, maybe talk to it if I can, and get a scan of its brain. Can you imagine what we could learn from its brain scans?" Her enthusiasm was almost infectious.

I had to shake my head as she swiped a wisp of hair from her face. "I know a few people that would rather learn from an autopsy of its brain, but that's a different story at the moment."

"It better be," she said firmly.

"You do realize that the head of the beast is the most dangerous place to be, even if this particular beast is intelligent," I said.

"Eh, that may be true," she responded, "but the head is also the best place to find information. Like you said, if he is intelligent, we need to talk to him."

"Oh, it's a 'he' and 'him' now?" I teased.

She blushed. "I was tired of calling him an 'it' or 'creature'."

I pulled back a bit and arched an eyebrow at her. "You really believe that the Puppet Master is sentient and can understand us, don't you?"

"Well," she said almost ashamedly, "yeah. I mean," she finally let go of my hand and turned around, paced a few feet down the tunnel, then returned. "I've been spending a lot of time thinking about this, it, everything. Why didn't he destroy the city, especially when you guys found the poison that hurt him?"

I had to admit that that very same thought had been weighing on my own mind, as well, during the past few weeks.

"What was he looking for with those tendrils?" she continued. "I mean, he had to be looking for something important, even while we were killing the dome, unless the tendrils were just a distraction or something."

That was a thought I hadn't contemplated before. What if the tendrils *had* simply been a distraction?

"So, yeah," she repeated as she placed her hand on my arm. "Yeah, I've been thinking about it. I want to know why and how the Puppet Master does what it does. Hell, I even want to know what its real name is, if it can tell me."

I noticed that she had switched her pronouns back

to 'it' instead of 'he' or 'him.' It didn't bother me, for we didn't know.

But did it mean she wasn't as sure as she sounded about this hypothesis? It was worth investigating, retrieving whatever information was useful for Rouhr.

And keeping her safe.

"Come on," she said, grabbing my hand again, heading off once more into the dark.

If she'd let me.

She didn't seem to be even remotely affected or concerned with holding my hand. It confused me. I had observed the human ritual of handholding, and it was generally reserved for parent and child, or someone that held a significant meaning to the other. Rokul and Tella held hands often, especially when she took him for walks in the park or to one of the neighborhood markets.

I was unaccustomed to someone holding my hand, and unsure of who held hands that were not family or lovers. Daphne and I were nothing to one another, right?

The sensation was...not unpleasant. I moved my thumb slightly over the back of her hand. Her skin was like silk. It was tempting to touch more of her, see more of her.

"Duck," she said. Grateful for her warning, I broke

free from my thoughts and barely missed a clump of roots that protruded from the ceiling of the tunnel.

"So, what are you going to do when we find whatever this is?" I asked. "I mean, besides try to scan its brain," I amended.

"I dunno," she shrugged. "Depends on whether or not he can communicate." She had switched pronouns again. "What about you?"

"What do you mean?" I asked.

She looked up at me as she continued holding my hand, slightly pulling me along. "I mean, if he is sentient and able to talk, what would you ask him?"

I shrugged. "I don't know," I lied. I did know. I would ask why it had attacked, what it was looking for, and why it hadn't simply come to talk to us from the very beginning.

"Liar," she said teasingly. "You know you want to ask it why and what?"

I smirked. "Well, if you know me so well, I'll just let you ask all the questions and I'll just stand there and look intimidating."

She did a double take. "You…you…you just cracked a joke!" she said, flabbergasted. "You actually cracked a joke. Oh. My. God. You're not a stuffy bag of muscle after all."

I shrugged. "And you're not entirely annoying."

"Oh," she gasped as she suddenly came to a halt.

"That...was that... really?" Her face dropped, her eyes showed pain, and she started to loosen her grip on my hand.

Skrell.

My stomach knotted, and I gently squeezed her hand. "I apologize. Sometimes," I tried to search for the right words, kicking myself. "Sometimes I forget that the humor I show to my brother and my teammates does not go over as well with others."

She looked at me, her expression still subdued. Suddenly, I felt terrible. I had caused her pain, and while I had originally begun not caring if her feelings were hurt, our short time together in the tunnels had shown her to be a woman of conviction and determination. I shouldn't think badly about someone simply because they wanted to do something, especially when that something had the potential to be beneficial to us all.

Without warning, she grinned from ear to ear. "You are adorable," she said. "You fell for it so hard."

I was...confused. What was she talking about?

"I'm sorry," she laughed. She got on her tiptoes and kissed me on the cheek, confusing me even more. She looked at my face and broke into tears as she laughed even harder. After finally catching her breath, she took a deep breath and explained. "I was messing with you. I know I can be annoying, it's one of my more endearing qualities once I make friends with someone. I was just teasing you."

I nodded as I licked my lips.

She had chosen to play a prank on me and I had fallen for it.

Nothing about this intriguing woman was fragile. A worthy mate --

I broke away from my thoughts as she smiled. "Come on," she said, yet again grabbing my hand.

This time, instead of letting her pull me, I decided to walk with her. It was a refreshing change of pace.

DAPHNE

The tunnels were disorienting. They snaked under the surface of the earth, cutting left and right randomly, and sometimes they even circled back to the same place we had been just a few minutes before. It was a complete maze and, even though Takar and I had been walking for over an hour now, I had no idea if we were any closer to the Puppet Master's nerve center.

"Okay." I stopped suddenly, and Takar bumped against me. "I think we might be lost."

"That's not good," he frowned. "The tunnels are a dangerous place. We can't keep walking around aimlessly, Daphne. If we get lost for good, who knows if we'll ever find a way out?"

"Thank you for the encouragement," I laughed. "You're a real optimistic, aren't you?"

"I prefer to be called a realist."

"Well, and I prefer to be someone who comes up with solutions," I threw back at him, already trying to think of something that would help us.

That was when I remembered the conversation Takar had had with his team members over the comms. "You brought a ground piercing sonar with you, right?"

"We did," he nodded, pursing his lips. "My team is probably setting it up as we speak."

"And there you have it...a solution!" I offered him a smile, but he just shook his head again. The man wasn't a fan of smiling, it seemed. Not that I could blame him. If someone had dragged me into such a dangerous situation against my will, I probably wouldn't be happy, either. "Can you call your team and ask them if they're ready? A layout of the caverns would really help."

Checking his wristwatch before grabbing his comms, he then gave me a slight nod. "Come in, team, this is Takar," he started, and the crackle of the comm's static returned, the sound of it filling the whole tunnel.

"What's up?" A voice said, and I recognized it as belonging to the person he'd spoken to before - Rokul. The familiarity between him and Takar seemed to indicate these two were close. Maybe even family. One thing was for sure: whoever was on the other side of

the comm sure as hell didn't seem to bother with proper military protocol. *"Can we start drilling already or what?"*

"No, no drilling," Takar replied. "What's the status on the ground sonar?"

"It's pretty much set and ready to go. We were just waiting for you to give the all clear before we power it up."

"Then let's get it running. These tunnels aren't easy to navigate, and the sooner we have a layout of this place the sooner we'll find what we're looking for."

"Copy that."

"Alright, that's done," Takar said, now turning to me. Leaning against the wall, he slumped down until he was sitting down on the ground. "It might take a few minutes, so I think we should gather our strength. We don't know how far we'll have to go."

"Fair enough," I said, sitting down right beside him. He seemed slightly uncomfortable with the fact that my body was close to his, but I couldn't tell if he was blushing. His skin was reddish-orange, after all, and I wasn't entirely sure if Skotans even blushed. Either way, it didn't really matter. Aside from the light coming out of our flashlights, the tunnels were dark and cramped. When I wasn't focused on my goal, and all the wonderful, interesting projects that could come out of finding the Puppet Master's nerve center, it was a little scary.

Just a touch.

I wanted my protector close to me.

I wasn't entirely sure if Takar would approve of me thinking of him as my protector, but that was how I saw him. And, even though we hadn't started our relationship on the right foot, he was starting to grow on me. He wasn't as boring and single-minded as most soldiers were, and he actually seemed curious about what I was trying to do. At first, I thought that was because of his devotion to the general, but now I was pretty sure he was just curious for some answers.

In that, we were alike.

After a few minutes of waiting, a voice finally came out of Takar's comm.

"*We're turning it on right now,*" it said. "*Stand by.*"

Takar and I remained sitting, waiting for the results of the sonar activity. Their equipment should be advanced enough that it wouldn't take more than just a few minutes for us to get a layout of the caverns, so we wouldn't have to wait long.

"What the hell...?" I muttered under my breath, feeling a slight vibration on the ground.

"I'm feeling it, too," Takar grumbled, jumping to his feet. I followed him, and that was when the soft vibration graduated into a strong rumbling sound. The earth beneath us started trembling, and I had to press one hand against the wall for support. Some of the smaller vines that jutted out of the walls here and there started slithering back into their holes, but most just thrashed around helplessly. They were trying to recede back into the walls, but it was as if they were disoriented.

"What the hell's going on?" I cried out, but the rumbling sound was so strong I doubted Takar could even hear me. Still, he closed in on me and draped one of his muscular arms over my shoulders, forcing me to stay beside him.

Dumbfounded, I watched as the vines went completely berserk around us. Their movements didn't seem intelligent anymore, and now they seemed wild and feral.

"Daphne! Watch out!" Takar shouted, spinning me around as I heard something crack behind me. I let out a scream of pain as a vine whipped me across my legs, and Takar just pulled me against his body to protect me from any further attacks.

It didn't make any sense.

Why would the vines be attacking me now?

Where was that intelligence? Why were the vines behaving as if they were...in pain?

That's it, I thought, *it has to be!*

"Tell them to shut the sonar off!" I cried out, but to no use. Takar was busy trying to fight against the vines in front of him, all of them lashing out randomly, and he couldn't hear me. "TAKAR!"

"Watch out!" he merely growled, pushing me out of the way as another vine dove straight toward us. As he did it, his comm unit fell from his belt and rolled toward me, stopping right before my boots.

Going down on one knee, I grabbed it with both hands and rolled to the side as another vine reached for me violently. I was about to speak into the comm when another vine hit me, this time straight across my back. I went down on the floor, dazed, but somehow managed to hold on to the comm. "Turn...it...off!" I managed to say, but my voice was so weak I doubted anyone heard me.

"Please repeat."

"TURN THE GODDAMN THING OFF!" I screamed at the top of my lungs, feeling so out of it that I let the comm roll off my tired fingers. It fell on the ground and, even though I tried to reach for it again, it simply slipped away as the earth kept on trembling.

I could do nothing but hope that Takar's team had heard me. Somehow, the sonar activity was causing pain to the vines...which meant that we needed that sonar turned off *fast*, or else this madness would never stop.

"It's okay...it's okay..." I repeated over and over again, trying to reach for the vines on the wall behind me. They kept on moving haphazardly, in a completely out of control fashion, and they just swatted my hands away as I tried to reach for them. "Please...we don't want to hurt you..." I insisted, doing my best to sound calm. If the vines could somehow pick up my mental state, I couldn't panic or I'd just make the situation even worse.

"Please...please...just calm down...no one means to hurt you. We're just—"

I was cut short by a loud sound coming right from underneath my feet, and I looked down just in time to see the earth cracking. It split open as the crack started to widen, the ground giving way to a deep darkness, and I found myself losing my balance.

I slipped into the darkness awkwardly, but somehow managed to hold on to the ledge. My fingers were hurting from the effort, and I felt beads of sweat roll down my forehead as I tried to hold on. I could already feel myself slipping, though, and this time there was no calming me down.

I was in full panic mode.

"Takar!" I tried to call him. "Takar, help!" He looked back over his shoulder just in time, and his eyes widened anxiously as he saw me hanging there. Gritting his teeth, determination taking over his face, he dashed toward me and jumped, holding me by the wrist just when my fingers let go.

"I've got you..." he said between hard breaths. "I've got you."

My wrist was slippery with sweat, though, and I could already feel myself slipping again. Two seconds later and I slipped away from Takar, my body immediately plunging into the darkness.

The last thing I saw was Takar diving after me.

TAKAR

Instinct took over as the ground opened up beneath Daphne. Muscles, tendons, ligaments, and electrical pulses instantly fired and worked together to launch me forward, rocketing my arm forward and forcing my hand to grab hold of Daphne's arm. The impact of my body on the ground knocked a bit of the air from my lungs, as well as loosened more of the ground beneath me.

The floor of the tunnel cracked, breaking against my body, then suddenly the ground was gone.

Daphne slipped away from my grip.

Not happening.

We fell through the darkness, all my focus on her wide eyes. I had to reach her.

Kicking my leg out, I caught the side of the wall, force adding speed to my descent. Reaching her, I pulled her into my chest, and with another kick, spun us around, activating my scales to help protect us from whatever rocks or debris lay below us.

I hit the ground, back first, and Daphne fell on top of me, knocking the remaining air from my lungs and bouncing my head off the ground.

I could feel my eyes twitching as I fought the oncoming darkness. I couldn't breathe, I couldn't move...the darkness was overwhelming everything. I felt as though I were swimming in oil, choking to death as I struggled to breathe. I felt my consciousness fading, fading away, spiraling into a blackness that would take away the pain.

No. No, I couldn't let myself give in. I fought the oncoming darkness, the ever-present push to just close my eyes and give in. I concentrated on the pain in my back, the pain in my ribs, the pain in my shoulder. I let the pain bring me back to consciousness, back to reality.

I gently, painfully, rolled Daphne off my chest.

She was breathing, her pulse was strong, but she was still unconscious. One of the vines must have whacked her.

I took in a breath of relief, gasping in pain as I

relished the sweet feeling of my lungs filling up again. My lungs weren't punctured, my ribs weren't broken, and I was so happy to know that I could breathe still.

I tentatively lifted myself up onto my elbows, then finally up to a seated position. My back felt as if I had been lying on it for weeks, but I knew that was simply the blood trying to work its way back through the veins and arteries, back into the muscles of my back, doing their natural healing process. Despite my scales, I was going to be bruised and sore for days.

I looked up. Make that, I was going to be bruised and sore for weeks. We must have fallen more than twenty feet. Where we lay now was at the floor of another tunnel, a smoother tunnel than the one we had traversed above. This one looked as though something had run back and forth through it thousands of times over the course of years. Except where we sat on debris, there were no indentations, no recesses, nothing in this tunnel except smooth surfaces, as if it were sanded down.

I looked back over to Daphne, reassured by the steady rise and fall of her chest. Pushing her hair away from her face, the mark on her temple where one of the vines had hit her was clear. She must have been nearly unconscious then, because when the ground broke, she fell like a toy doll.

Just before the ground broke entirely, Daphne had grabbed my comm unit. I searched for it, but couldn't find it anywhere. I dug up some of the broken tunnel, flinging clods of dirt and rock away so I wouldn't waste time looking under them again thinking I missed something.

I found it in the dirt. It was bruised and damaged, battered enough that it likely would only get a signal once we got closer to the surface. It wasn't strong enough in its damaged state to communicate through all the rock. With a sudden thought, I checked my gear.

One of the blasters was bent, useless now. Luckily, my other blaster was fine, as was my knife.

I wasn't so lucky with my tablet or my tracking unit. The tablet screen was shattered, small pieces of it sticking up or falling out as I held it up. My tracking unit was cracked in half, utterly useless now.

What had caused the vines to go berserk like that? Could it have been the sonar scan Rokul and Sylor had conducted? Was it possible that the sonar frequency hurt the Puppet Master? That was valuable information, and something that I needed to get to the general.

But first, I had to get us out of here. Unfortunately, with no communication capabilities, and no map of the tunnel system, getting out was going to be an adventure.

I looked back at Daphne. If it hadn't been for her and her impulsiveness, I would never have been here. I would have been back in Nyheim, walking patrol.

And maybe, just a little bit bored.

I would have been walking patrol, having zero clue as to how big the Puppet Master was, how it seemed to be willing to communicate, and that our sonar scanners could cause it pain.

I slowly moved closer to her, my body already getting stiff from the fall, and reached out. I carefully moved my arms under her and gently lifted her back towards me. I tried my best to make her as comfortable as possible against me while still supporting her so she could breathe.

"I wish you could tell me if this was okay," I said quietly. "I've never been terribly good at being the soft and gentle type. I'm sorry, Daphne. I'm sorry for not being more diligent about keeping you safe." I looked at her and wondered if my words were being heard. There had been countless studies showing that, even in a coma, you could hear the people around you. Doctors and scientists had done the scans that showed the parts of the brain that registered hearing and understanding lit up, even while comatose. However, it also showed little to no activity in the memory portion of the brain, depending on how bad your level of unconsciousness was.

"I…I think you can hear me, but I don't know if you'll remember any of what I say," I whispered to her, pushing a strand of hair out of her face as I did so. "I'm sure you figured out that I didn't want you to be down here, and I certainly didn't want to be dragged down here by you. I should have tried harder to stop you, to keep you in one place where we would have been safer.

"But, somehow, you infected me with your enthusiasm. I don't think I have ever seen someone so enthusiastic…no, enthusiasm is the wrong word." I cursed myself for making that mistake. I was better than this. "Optimism. You were so optimistic about this half-processed plan of yours, if you could even say it was half-processed, that I found it difficult to contradict you.

"I…I've seen members of my team, and members of another team, fall for the women that they've come to work with, and they've all shown enthusiasm, and optimism, and even glee at the work that they were doing," I continued. "But none of those women, at least in my limited experience with them, have ever been so…so…so headstrong and bullheaded as you. You let your optimism and excitement of researching this creature get the best of you, and somehow, I felt a small bit of that.

"I liked it," I admitted to her unconscious form. "I

liked feeling that optimism that something could be done. It…even if I wasn't prepared to admit it, it pushed me to follow you."

Where was any of this coming from? I never allowed myself to be so exposed. Not even my own brother, who knew everything about me, was privy to this level of exposure. I told him everything, he knew of my love of study, my true chosen path to enter the world of science—even military science—and my fears and worries, just as I knew his.

But never had I ever allowed myself to feel as vulnerable around him as I felt around her.

Not even when our tribe and city were obliterated in the Xathi attack. Rokul never spoke of it, but I knew that the destruction of our home, and the loss of our entire family, our tribe, weighed on him, as it did on me.

Something about this woman brought out, at least at this moment, parts of me that I had reserved only for myself.

I stroked her forehead, smoothing back the soft strands of hair that had long ago fallen from her bun. I'd wanted to do that from the first moment we met.

"I…" I chuckled a bit at my own hesitation, my own cowardliness.

How could I *not* speak right now? "I don't know if

I've ever met someone that's as nice as you are. You're nice to the creature that we're trying to kill. You're even nice to me, and I've been nothing but angry with you."

Something caught my eye. I glanced down and saw her eyelids flutter, almost as if she were trying to keep her eyes closed. I stayed quiet and stared, and watched as one eyelid lifted, almost imperceptibly.

The corner of her mouth started to rise.

"What the zet?" I asked, the anger only barely held in check. "You're awake?"

She opened both of her eyes, not even bothering to look the slightest bit embarrassed by her action, or non-action. "What?" she asked innocently.

I had visions of throwing her off me and leaving her behind, letting her die in this rekking underground abyss. "You were *pretending* to be unconscious and listening to me speak?"

She nodded, her head on my leg as her body rested against me. "Only for the last bit, I think. I didn't want to interrupt." She smothered a giggle as I glared at her.

"Oh, stop that. You ended up on a protective detail that you didn't sign up for and you've done a terrific job, okay? I'm still alive, I'm only a little sore, and we're doing good. You are doing fantastic, okay?" She struggled a bit to push herself up. "Help me up. Please?"

I helped her sit up. She wobbled a bit when she tried to rise on her own, but she eventually sat by herself. I ran my hands over her limbs to make sure there was nothing broken, trying to keep my movements and thoughts professional. Disciplined.

She was quiet while I checked her over, and I was left with my reeling thoughts. I was happy to see that she wasn't hurt any further, and I was surprised at that, considering I was still angry at her for essentially lying to me.

Or was I?

Kneeling next to her, all thoughts disappeared as her face came close to mine. Her tongue darted out, licking her lips, and for a moment I froze, transfixed.

Micron by micron, I moved closer to her, watching her eyes darken, so close I could hear her breath grow ragged, see the subtle flare of her nostrils. Gently wrapping one arm around her back, the other hand winding in her hair, I brushed my lips against hers.

Sweet, soft.

Indescribable.

I lingered, luxuriating in the feel of her, then leaned back to break the connection.

Or started to.

Daphne moved forward faster, her arms winding around my neck, that tempting, tentative tongue teasing at the seam of my lips.

For a long moment, we stayed quiet, our mouths far too occupied for words.

Finally, she ended it. "We should get going if we want to figure this thing out and find a way out of here."

The only movement left within me, other than my heart threatening to break through my ribs, was a nod.

DAPHNE

I followed Takar down into the twisting tunnels, my eyes focused on his figure. He was tall and muscular, and despite there being an edge to him, it only added to the attraction. Even though he was wearing his tactical gear, I could still see the contours of his toned muscles under his clothing. And there was something about his red skin that was so damn alluring.

It was still weird to think of him like that, but after that kiss…it was impossible not to. I still felt the pressure of his mouth on mine, and it was hard focusing on the task at hand when all I wanted was a repeat of that kiss. It didn't help, of course, that we were completely alone. That just ensured my brain kept on coming up with different scenarios, all of them involved me falling into his arms.

I didn't even know entirely why I had kissed him in the first place. It had just felt right at the time, and I had acted on impulse. After listening to him speak with such abandon, to hear a man like him open up...I simply didn't have it in me to resist my growing attraction any more.

But I was more than just attracted, I was curious about him, too. I had thought he was nothing but a brute on a government leash, but I was slowly coming to realize he was so much more than that. There were layers to him, and I wanted to start peeling them back.

He was protective and caring, and even though he wanted to do his job, he didn't abandon all common sense just so he could follow his orders. More than that, he was as smart as he was curious, and he seemed genuinely determined to find a solution to the Puppet Master problem.

But there was still a lot I didn't know about him.

"You don't talk much, do you?" I asked him, earning a casual glance from him. We had time to kill while we walked, so I figured I could pepper him with questions. Maybe that way I'd find out more about him. "Except when I'm unconscious, that is. Do you want me to pretend I'm asleep or something? I could do that."

"What do you want to talk about?" he asked me,

never slowing down his pace and purposefully ignoring the way I was teasing him.

I kept on following after, struggling a bit to keep up with him, but I didn't complain: the sooner we found the Puppet Master's brain, the better. Besides, now that we had no way of communicating with the outside, time was of the essence. Unless we found a way out, we were probably going to starve down here.

"I don't know," I replied, shrugging. Then, smiling, I decided to mimic the voice of a famous Nyheim holonews presenter. "Tell me about yourself. Who is the real Takar?"

"And what exactly do you want to know?"

"Anything," I insisted. I was slowly starting to realize that a conversation with Takar was like trying to open a tin can with your bare hands, but I wasn't going to let that stop me. "What do you like doing?"

"I'm a soldier."

"No," I laughed. "I mean, outside of work. Or is being a soldier your hobby?"

"Of course not," he replied. "Being a soldier is my job."

"But you must have a life outside of work."

"I don't."

I sighed. I should pretend to be unconscious again; maybe that way he'd start talking to me. I had only meant it as a joke before, but I was now starting to see the merits in such a stupid idea. "Why did you become a soldier, then?" I insisted once more. "Did you always want to become one? Is that why you enlisted under General Rouhr?"

"Most people don't become soldiers because it's their dream," he shrugged, not even bothering to look back at me. "A few are born fighters, that's true, but most soldiers fall into that role out of necessity."

"I see," I nodded. "So, you became a soldier because of the Xathi? Did they invade your homeworld?"

"In a way," he admitted, and this time he finally stopped and turned around to face me. "The Xathi obliterated most of my tribe, and they laid waste to my city. But it was my older brother, Rokul, that was hell bent on fighting them. I just followed after him to make sure he didn't get killed."

I opened my mouth to say something...but I didn't.

I had no idea of what I should say. I had seen how savage the Xathi could be, and I couldn't even begin to imagine how it would feel to lose everything at the hands of those creatures. When the Xathi started their attacks, I had been lucky: I had escaped the war unscathed, and both my parents had managed to survive. Most people I knew had lost someone, and I was one of the lucky few whose whole family had survived.

"I'm sorry," I finally managed to say. "Was Rokul the one on the comms?"

"Yeah, he's the dumbass coordinating the efforts on the surface. He's probably losing it right now, thinking we're dead or something. Which we will be, unless we find a way out of this place."

"Wow, you really are an optimist, no doubt about it," I chuckled, doing my best to lighten the mood. "Alright, let's try this...if you hadn't followed your brother into the military, what do you think you'd be doing? Would you be an engineer? A pilot? A gardener?"

He paused for a moment, his eyes on mine, and I could tell he was trying to think of an answer. "I don't know," he merely told me, and I felt my heart tighten at such a response.

The Xathi had robbed Takar of a life, it seemed, and his world had shrunk so much that it could only accommodate the military. I felt sad for him—the way I saw it, there was nothing worse than not having dreams. "After a while, I never really thought about a life outside the military. I just went wherever my brother went. Even though he's older than me, I've always been the responsible one...and it's my duty to ensure his safety."

"That takes character," I smiled. What I really wanted to do was give him a big hug, but I stopped myself from doing it. I knew he wasn't the emotional type, but I wasn't sure if I'd be able to stop my own tears from coming. "You must have a big heart, Takar."

"I'm a Skotan. Biologically speaking, our hearts are bigger than human ones. So, yes, I have a big heart."

"That's not what I meant," I said, not sure if I should laugh or give him a frown. "It's just a human expression...it means that you care for others, and that you are a kind person. It means that you are...*good*."

"I..." He trailed off, and then scratched his chin and nodded to himself. "Thank you, Daphne. I appreciate your words."

"No need to thank me," I smiled, reaching for him and holding his hand. "Just stating the obvious."

Sweet man.

Sweet, big-hearted man was slowly giving me answers.

And the more I found, the more I wanted - needed - to know.

TAKAR

"Being a neuroscientist wasn't my first plan," she was telling me as we tried to find a way back up to where we fell from. We had come to find out, the tunnel we had fallen into wasn't a completed tunnel. In one direction, it stopped maybe twenty yards from where we landed, so it forced us back to the other direction in hopes of finding a way out, or back to where we fell, or to the brain of the Puppet Master. "I started off wanting to explore space, you know? I guess every kid does." She glanced up at me. "Until recently, we didn't even know there were more than other human colonies out there. Surprise!"

She went on to tell me that being a space explorer ended up being what she called a pipe-dream, since the citizens on Ankau didn't have a space program. That seemed a bit odd to me. They landed here using a starship, so why wouldn't they have a way to get back off the planet if they needed to? Actually, the more I thought about it, the more I realized I'd never even seen the ship they originally landed in. Where was it?

I didn't get an opportunity to ask. Daphne was still explaining how her own pathway through life changed. "Then, after I got over the space explorer kick, I wanted to become an explorer on this planet. I wanted to study everything about the planet. I always wondered why we only populated this continent, but then I thought about it a little and realized that we didn't have enough people to spread out, at least not yet."

It made sense. A small population would only be capable of exploring and inhabiting a relatively small area. It would also be prudent to keep that smaller population of people relatively close to one another in case anyone needed anything, to establish trade, and to allow different options for living and for study.

I was glad that she was doing all of the talking as we searched. I was uncomfortable with sharing things about myself. I just never felt the need to divulge too much about who I was and what I was feeling. If people needed to know something about me, I would tell them.

And right now, I wanted to know more about her.

Everything.

"So, because of that incident, I decided to go into

neuroscience. I wanted to know why the brain did what it did. I mean," she squeezed my hand as she looked up at me. "I know we've got hundreds of years of study on the brain already done, but not from here, you know? The atmosphere is a little different here, the water is a little different, so I figured that it might affect brains differently. Don't you think?"

I nodded. She waited a moment, and when I didn't say anything, she sort of frowned. "Are you even paying attention to me?"

"Yes," I answered. "And I believe that your reasoning for thinking that the environment of Ankau will have a different effect on the brain than your original planet is sound."

"Thank you," she smiled sheepishly. "I was worried you weren't listening to me." Then she continued, talking about how she thought that if there really were environmental effects on the human brain, that could help her be a pioneer in the scientific field.

I was listening to the sound of her voice without the words she was saying. I liked hearing her voice. It was soothing. It reminded me of what it felt like to hold her. To press her body close to me.

"Stop," I said as I stopped walking. Daphne looked back at me, a look of concern on her face. "Do you recognize any of this?" I asked.

"Should I?" she asked in return.

I nodded. We were back in the tunnel that led to where we had fallen. "Follow me," I said, grabbing her hand. I gently pulled her along behind me as we walked down the tunnel. Soon enough, we were back to where the floor had broken away.

"Wow," she said when she finally got a good look at the distance we had fallen. She looked back at me in admiration. "Are you sure you're okay?"

I nodded. "I'm fine. I'll be a little sore, but that's all. Look," I said, pointing at what looked to be scrape marks on the tunnel walls. "I think that the vines tried to retreat down this tunnel and were reacting erratically in their haste."

She nodded as she released my hand and studied the scrapes on the walls. "They must have been responding to the sonic frequency of your sonar scanner," she said.

That was exactly what I had thought. She truly was a smart woman.

"You know what that means, don't you?" she asked me, clapping her hands together in excitement.

"Not exactly," I answered, unable to catch on to her sudden burst of bubbly enthusiasm.

She was exasperated. "Oh, come on. If it struggles with sonic frequencies, that means it has a tremendously sophisticated and sensitive sense of hearing."

"Okay," I nodded. I still didn't get where she was going with it.

Daphne had said that there was a chance the Puppet Master wasn't a plant, but a creature, or animal, of some sort.

"So, it's not a plant. It generates its own heat, something plants do not do," I started to summarize. She nodded. "It has incredibly sensitive hearing, something most plants don't have," I continued. "And it seems to be protective of you, something plants aren't normally known for."

"Exactly," she responded.

"What do you think it is then?" I asked.

She shook her head and shrugged. "I don't know. Not yet, anyway." She turned to study the tunnel walls again for a moment. "But if I can get to the head, maybe snag a quick brain scan, I can try to figure it out."

I nodded. "Then we should keep moving."

"Wait," she said as she looked at me, surprise evident on her face. "You believe me?"

I had to give her a sort of half-shrug. "Not entirely. I still believe that whatever the Puppet Master is, it's a danger to all of us. However," I said quickly as she opened her mouth to argue, "I agree that we need to study it in order to know how we're going to deal with it."

"We're not going to 'deal with it'," she said, imitating my tone perfectly. "It's intelligent. It has to be."

"Why?" I asked.

"Because," she said, "if it weren't intelligent, both of us would be dead right now. And, if you really think about it...I mean *really* think about it...only an intelligent creature would have done what it's done so far."

"Explain," I ordered...nicely.

She arched an eyebrow, then proceeded to explain her reasoning. "If it wasn't intelligent, it would have simply destroyed Duvest, Nyheim, and the other places it attacked."

She was back to that argument again.

"I mean, please, think it through. Yes, there was a lot of damage," she admitted. "And a few deaths, but did the vines ever directly kill anyone? Like, purposefully and maliciously kill any of the people that died?"

I shook my head. She had been right. The Puppet Master's attacks had not been malicious and purposely deadly. As a matter of fact, the deaths in Nyheim were inadvertent results of the dome being built over us.

"Do you see where I'm going with this?" she asked. "It didn't kill anyone on purpose. I looked at the reports. The people that died in Einhiv were either crushed by parts of falling buildings or because they fell in the holes. In Duvest, it was mostly the same. The only exception was the driver that got scared and drove right into a downed power line."

That had been a terrible site to investigate. Power had to be shut down to that entire section of town, and even then, the vehicle still had residual electrical energy running through it. The poor driver never stood a chance.

The same could be said in Nyheim. An elderly gentleman had died when the power went down and the machinery helping him breathe shut down. Another was killed when a piece of building fell on his head, snapping his neck and spine.

Still, I wasn't entirely sold on her theory.

"I can see that you're not buying it," she said. If she continued to read my face and mind like this, there would be little to no need for anymore conversation between the two of us. "But none of the deaths were intentional, they were circumstantial, a result of the chain reaction of events from his actions."

"I do understand your reasoning, and it does fit with your theory," I said. "My concern is that it has no intention of trying to live *with* us instead of against us."

"Then how do you explain how he wrapped the vines around me in order to protect me?" she demanded. "When you pulled out your blaster and shot the vines, it didn't attack you, did it? No," she said, answering for me. "It protected me. It thought you were trying to hurt me, so it wrapped vines around me in order to protect me."

"What about what it did in that little town outside the forest? The one close to what used to be Fraga?" I asked, referring to the attack that happened when Iq'her had followed Stasia and tried to put a stop to her brother's anti-alien group.

The rumors of that attack had swept through the city.

She threw her arms up in the air. "Not everything follows the pattern, I know. But until we find out more, maybe we can't figure out what the real pattern is."

"Okay, okay," I said, my hands held up to show I was 'surrendering' the fight. "I'll give it, whatever it is, a chance."

Daphne smiled at me and turned to make her way down the tunnel. We made our way around the hole we had fallen down and restarted our trek through the tunnels.

I wasn't completely convinced, not yet. Too many things were unknown, and it was better to be safe and prepared.

But I would be on her side, protecting her, no matter what we found.

Whether she liked it or not.

DAPHNE

"See?" I asked Takar with a smile. I was down on one knee, caressing a small vine as it wrapped itself around my wrist gently. It caressed me back, its tip softly brushing against the open palm of my hand. "It likes me."

"You don't know that for sure," Takar said. "Maybe it's just testing, seeing if you're easily eaten."

I stuck my tongue out at him, but despite his words, he seemed to be impressed with the dynamic I had established with the vines. I wasn't sure if they actually felt about me in the way a human would like someone, but they seemed to have grown fond of me.

After all, the vines had protected me from Takar when they thought he was going to shoot me, and they always reacted positively whenever I reached out and touched them.

"Yes, I know for a fact that they like me," I laughed, my eyes never leaving the small vine in front of me. As I got up, it slid back from my wrist, but it remained swaying back and forth, almost like a leaf being tossed by the wind. "I'm not entirely sure what the Puppet Master is, but you have to admit...it recognizes me. And I think I might have established a bond with it."

"I still don't understand why that would happen."

"Me neither," I admitted. "But it seems like the vines respond to more than just my voice...they respond to my touch, as well. In fact, that might be the best way to communicate with the Puppet Master. Maybe the vines have only attacked people in the cities because everyone reacts violently the moment they see them. People get scared, and that just makes them become defensive."

It was still a working theory, but I had been gently stroking every vine I saw on our trek through the tunnels and I always managed to elicit a positive reaction. Even though I knew I had to be cautious, I was no longer afraid of the Puppet Master. I was merely intrigued by it.

"Do you really think it has a brain?" Takar asked me, still eyeing the vine in front of us with distrust. One sudden movement and I was pretty sure Takar wouldn't hesitate before reaching for his blaster. He didn't strike me as being the typical trigger-happy soldier, but something had shifted down here.

"Maybe a nerve center of some kind?"

"Hard to know," I sighed, resting my hand on the wall for support. My body was growing heavy, and I was still feeling slightly dizzy. Even though I hadn't broken anything when I fell through that hole, my body was complaining from the fall. "But I don't think these vines can stand alone. Think of them as the arms and legs of the Puppet Master. They're just an extension of what he is."

"If that's true, then he must be enormous," he said. "The vines have been attacking—or, sorry, appearing—in different points of the region. From Nyheim to Fraga, we've spotted them pretty much everywhere. Do you really think something of that magnitude is possible?"

"I'm not sure," I nodded, pursing my lips. "But if I'm right and it's a single creature we're talking about, then yeah...its size must be impressive..." I trailed off then, my thoughts bouncing off the walls of my skull at random. I was becoming too damn exhausted to even think straight. Leaning back against the wall, I closed my eyes for a second and raked one hand over my face.

"Daphne, are you alright?" Takar asked me, his voice distant and muffled. God, I was feeling so dizzy I wouldn't be surprised if I simply collapsed. It didn't help that there was a hole in my stomach. I had had breakfast eight hours ago, sure. But the physical exertion and lack of supplies meant that my body was starting to weaken.

"I'm fine, I'm fine," I lied, but I couldn't stop myself from slumping down to the ground, exhaustion finally taking me over. "I'm just tired."

"Let's stop for a while," he said, and this time I didn't have a doubt: that was an order, and Takar wouldn't take no for an answer. "You might've hit your head harder than I realized when you fell, Daphne."

Going down one knee, he carefully placed one hand on my face and forced me to turn my head to the side. Examining me with the flashlight, he took his time as he seemingly felt every single inch of my head. "I see nothing else," he finally concluded, "but I still think it's best to rest for a couple of hours."

"It's already night up on the surface, isn't it?" I managed to ask him, and he just nodded patiently. No wonder I was feeling so damn exhausted. I had barely slept on the way to the crater, and Takar and I had never stopped to rest since we had started our trek down into the tunnels.

"I'm going to keep watch, so you can sleep," he told me, sitting right beside me and draping one arm over my shoulders. I didn't think it was fair for him to keep watch while I conked out, but I was feeling so tired that I didn't even have the strength to protest. I just snuggled up against him, laying my head on his chest, and closed my eyes.

I was about to drift off to sleep when my stomach roared, doing it so loudly my eyelids fluttered open in an instant. Goddammit, I was starving. I had left all the food I had brought inside the hovercraft, and I hadn't had anything to eat in hours. Oh, what I wouldn't give for a simple snack bar!

"Sorry," Takar whispered softly. "I don't have any food with me."

"It's not your fault, Takar," I told him, the warmth of his body seeping into mine. "I should've planned this better. You were right. I was a bit of a fool, wasn't I?"

"Scientists need to be fools." Gently running one hand through my hair, he laid his lips against my forehead. "Besides, I was the fool in this situation. I should've listened to you when you came to the inquiry office. You had ideas, you wanted to contribute...I should've taken you more seriously. But I didn't, and so you felt you had to come here all by yourself."

"Stop acting like a martyr, will you?" I chuckled, punching his arm. "We're in this together now. It doesn't matter whose fault it is...what matters is that we get out of here alive. And with some answers, too."

"You're hungry and thirsty and exhausted...and you still haven't given up on the Puppet Master?"

"What can I say?" I asked him, looking up into his eyes. "I don't give up that easily. Not on anything."

"Yes, you definitely don't—"

He fell silent the moment we heard something move in the darkness, a rustling sound that echoed through the tunnel, and he reached for his blaster almost immediately. He pointed it at the darkness, his finger already on the trigger, when a single vine slithered into view. It rose up until it was level with our eyes, and only then did I realize it was weighed down with fruit.

"Impossible," Takar muttered, and I just smiled as I picked up the fruits.

"It's taking care of us," I whispered, handing Takar one of the fruits. I didn't know exactly what type of fruit it was, but its surface was red and smooth, almost like a blend between a peach and an apple. When I took a bite out of it, the sweetness made me close my eyes and I moaned softly. "It tastes so freaking good."

"We should be careful." Takar eyed the fruit warily. "What if it's poisoned?"

"Aha!" I mumbled around another bite. "Then you agree that the Puppet Master is intelligent?"

He rolled his eyes, sniffing carefully at the fruit.

"Besides," I added, "if he wanted to kill us, I'm pretty

sure there are about twenty more direct methods. Massive vines, remember?"

"True," Takar agreed, then finally took a bite of his own.

We were so hungry that we didn't say a word to each other as we devoured the fruit, it's juice easing my parched throat. Afterward, once my stomach was no longer busy devouring itself, I laid my head against Takar's shoulder and then...

Then it was lights out.

TAKAR

There had been no point in staying in bed, not with the children trying to be quiet. Their attempts to be silent were essentially an invitation to noise. I patted Daphne on the backside. "It's time to wake up. The little monsters are probably hungry and about to try to make their own breakfast."

She moaned, swiped weakly at me, and buried her head in her pillow. I chuckled, leaned over and kissed the back of her neck. "Come on, you know you'll hate yourself if you sleep in again," I said as I kissed my way to her ear.

She giggled as I played with her ear. "Stop it," she laughed as she tried to push me away.

"You really want me to?" I asked coyly.

She rolled over, a look of lust in her eyes. "No." She reached up and pulled me in for a passionate kiss.

No matter how many years it had been, I never stopped wanting her. Needing her. All the time.

We made love, gently at first. Every time, sliding into Daphne was like coming home. Every slow, deep thrust like finding another part of myself, of my soul.

But as we spiraled into our desires, we began to get rougher. Nastier. Daphne's body contorted in her pleasure but she gave as good as she got, climbing on top of me on more than one occasion and riding me with wild abandon. We finished and lay back on the bed, exhausted and satisfied. And covered ourselves only a few moments before the children came bounding into the room. They jumped onto the bed as we quickly finished covering ourselves.

"Mommy! Daddy!" they both yelled as they bounced around us, their laughter infectious.

"Ungh, ungh," I grunted in laughter. "You two better stop bouncing on daddy's bladder before we have an accident in here."

They stopped bouncing long enough to look at one another before yelling out together, "TICKLE DADDY!" They both jumped on me, trying to tickle me through the blankets.

Our tickle fight lasted a few minutes before we finally got the children to leave with the promise of breakfast and playtime outside.

I looked at Daphne and marveled at the beauty of her face, and remembered exactly how beautiful her body was, the years together only adding to my adoration.

These were the mornings that I looked forward to, a day meant just for the family, just for Daphne and me and the home we'd made. She joined me in the bathroom as I was brushing my teeth. "Hey, tiger," she said as she patted me on the butt. I quickly reached behind me and grabbed her, bringing her close to me. She reached her arms around my torso, hugging me close.

"So," I said with a smile, the toothbrush dangling from my mouth. "What's on the agenda for today?"

She peeked her head around me and smiled into the mirror. "Well," she whispered seductively. She ran her hand down my torso, not stopping until she could grab me and tease me a little. "Maybe we can wear the kids out quickly and put them down for a nap, then we can make another one."

I SNORTED as I jerked awake. We were still sitting on the tunnel floor, right where we had been, however long ago it was that I'd told Daphne to rest.

I was confused. It must have been a dream, but it was so real, so vivid. I had never had a dream that felt like that, like another life, just waiting for me to close my eyes.

It should have been disturbing.

Yet, it was…comfortable.

The only thing that truly bothered me about the

entire episode was that I had fallen asleep. I'm not a big sleeper in the first place, living on an average of three to four hours a night every day since my brother and I joined the military.

So, in order for me to have fallen asleep, I was either drugged or much more tired than I would have thought.

The vines had brought us fruits to eat, almost as if they knew we were hungry and without food. This was going to be yet another thing that Daphne was going to use in her argument that the Puppet Master was an intelligent and powerful being. I sighed and chuckled lightly.

I sort of enjoyed those little arguments, it showed the passion and tenacity within her blood. *She* was intelligent, that was without a doubt, and she was confident in her thoughts, even if she didn't have any proof to defend them.

I looked at her, her head still on my shoulder as she slept. She looked so…she looked the same as she had in the dream.

That dream had suggested that we were together, life mates, and that we had been so for years. Long enough to have children that were a few years in age.

She had that same wisp of hair in her face again. She should really figure out a way to deal with that. I reached over and carefully moved the strand back to where it belonged. I ran my fingers through her hair, causing her to rub her head against my shoulder. It felt good to have her against me.

I smiled at her and thought back to the dream. In it, we had two children, one boy and one girl, both with the same colored skin as Daphne, but with my orange hair and a hint of scales. Their muscles were already beginning to show, even though they were only a few years in age. The intelligence and joy in their eyes were unmistakable.

I found myself wanting those children in my world, as part of my life. I felt as if something was missing, as if a body part was missing or not working properly without them here, next to me at this very moment.

I looked at her face, so peaceful in sleep, and remembered what her body looked like in my dream. I let my eyes travel down her body, letting my memory of the dream see through the clothes. There were vines covering her from her navel down to her feet. I instinctively reached down to pull them off and found that they weren't wrapped around her, merely covering her.

They were keeping her warm.

I swear, I thought to myself, it's like this thing likes her. Which isn't terribly shocking, everyone seemed to like her.

Sylor and Rokul loved that she stole my comm unit

and used it, so they were already liking her. I'm pretty sure that Trevor and the other two guards thought nice things about her as well. I even liked her.

I chuckled to myself at the thought of it. As much as I tried to remain my own person, distinct and separate, despite my closeness to my brother, I still ended up like him.

He had fallen for a human female, and if that dream was any kind of predictor of the future, I would as well. Perhaps I already had and simply didn't know it.

I leaned down and kissed her on the forehead.

She moaned again, then turned her head and looked up at me. "Hey," she said quietly.

"Hey," I said in return. There was a different look in her eyes than before. It was a look of peace, and complete trust...mixed with a little bit of...

I was unable to complete the thought as she reached up, put her hand on my neck, and pulled me down to her.

We kissed. Still gentle, but deeper this time. Connected.

I felt her soft lips on mine again and this time I didn't hold back. I pushed my face closer to her and our mouths opened up. Her tongue slipped into my mouth and began to attack mine in a mischievous fashion.

Everything Daphne had exhibited up till now made

its way through her kiss. Her confidence. Her impetuousness. Her lust for life.

And it came to me. I wanted more of her, to see more of her, to know her better.

And then I just lost myself in her kiss.

I couldn't dream of anything more perfect than that moment.

DAPHNE

The kiss we shared was fantastic, and comforting. It somehow just felt...right. I didn't really know how to explain it any other way.

I mean, yes, it did come across as a clichéd description, but things become a cliché when they're true.

We had stopped kissing a while ago, but I wanted to do it again. His arms holding me just made my blood race through my veins. I wanted nothing more than to feel him hold me again...okay, maybe one thing more.

I had to admit that while I was kissing him, I had definitely been thinking about what his lips and tongue would feel like over the rest of my body...and what something else would feel like being rubbed all over my body.

I felt the blood rush to my cheeks as I imagined his thick member touching me, penetrating me. It was…entrancing.

I had to think of something else. Quickly. "So, you said that you had a brother."

"That's right," he nodded. "Older."

"Oh, so did he tease you and beat you up a lot when you were kids?" I asked. I was trying to take my mind off his lips and his…

"He tried," Takar laughed. "Before I grew into my body, as my father used to say, Rokul was the more powerful of the two of us. But once I started to show my size, our brotherly battles started to equalize."

"Oh," I nodded. I wasn't sure what else to say really. I didn't have siblings, and while occasionally I wondered what I was missing in that bond, it's hard to miss something you've never had.

We started talking a little more about what I did at the hospital, about what he did in the city, and just random things. It was easy to talk to him. Hell, I had told him things about my past that I never told guys on a first date, or even after a month into the relationship. And I had told him a few hours into knowing him.

While we talked, part of my mind wandered. When I had been asleep, I had an insanely vivid dream. It felt so real that, when I woke up, I had to concentrate hard to control my breathing and to not throw myself at him.

The dream had been so vivid that I could have sworn that between my legs I could still feel what it was like to have him inside me. Stretching me.

Swallowing hard to bring my concentration back to the conversation, I looked up at him while we walked and talked.

He looked relaxed, as if all our conflict earlier had never happened. His posture before now had always been rigid and straight. He had always seemed to be annoyed with me, and I had to grudgingly admit that I had been a bit of a pain in the ass. It was in my nature… I always figured that it was the best way to figure out who was really willing to put up with me and who was just there because of either my job or my parents.

Not that I should have worried about it with Takar. He had never met my parents and he never seemed the type to care about a person's position.

Except in the dream, and the position he had worried about was a position that had made me nearly scream in pleasure.

In the dream, we had been in the same bed, in a house that had four bedrooms. We were trying to sleep in, but our kids…a little boy and girl…were attempting to be quiet. So, of course that meant that they were making a ton of noise that could have woken up a deaf dead man.

We had joked around a little, lovingly teased one

another, then snuck in a quick session of oh-my-fucking-lord-this-feels-good love making. At least that's what it started as. But just thinking back to the vividness of the sex in the dream made me blush. I was a wanton woman with Takar, mounting him and taking myself to paradise shamelessly. And he used me for his pleasure, while shooting me higher and higher. I had just barely gotten my panties and shirt back on when the kids burst into the room and started a tickle fight with us.

We were a family, with two beautiful kids, and everything just seemed right. I knew that we were able to talk to one another about anything and everything. We supported one another in everything we did, and loved one another. I could trust him to do the dishes or cook dinner when I was running late, just like I knew I could trust him to care for the kids and never cheat on me.

He could trust me all the same, as well as trust me to do things to him that would make him tremble right before he lost control…in a good way.

It was the dream life, and when I woke up and realized that it really had been just a dream, I nearly cried.

He had kissed me on the forehead, bringing me out of the dream world and into reality. I knew that I had to kiss him, so I did. It didn't even seem like much of an issue to kiss him, like it was something that we had already done thousands of times.

Should I tell him that?

I thought as we walked. Should I tell him about the dream, about how we were a family and we were together in all ways? What if he didn't feel the same way as I did? Holy shit…did I really feel something now because of that dream?

I looked at him, taking all of him in with my eyes as we walked, as he talked. I honestly couldn't say what he was talking about at that moment, my mind was barely on point. However, I guess enough of my mind was paying attention that I was able to answer or comment, and it sounded coherent.

Who the hell am I and where did I get this magical power?

I stifled a chuckle, pretending that it was a small cough instead. I didn't want him to think I was crazy.

But did I really have feelings for him, aside from the physical attraction? Was I just remembering how I felt in the dream or was it real?

I forced my attention onto reality, onto where we were and what we were trying to do. We were below the surface, in a crazy maze of tunnels, looking for something that controlled the plants above.

I wondered if we…and by 'we' I meant 'I'…had made the right decision to come down here.

I looked around at the tunnel we were in. The rock of it was different than before...it was grayer than the brown from before. It looked stronger and thicker than the rock above us. It made sense. I knew that the deeper into the planet we got and the closer we got to the molten core, the thicker, darker, and stronger the rock should become.

Now I was confused. I had officially confused myself trying to remember something about rocks that I had learned in the eighth grade. I shook my head and just concentrated on walking and talking with Takar.

"What about you?" he asked me. I couldn't remember the conversation topic. I racked my brain trying to remember, then it snapped in clearly. We had been talking about the anti-alien group and he was asking me what I thought about the prison they were trying to set up.

I shrugged. "I don't know, really. If we set up the prison and only keep the anti-alien people there, won't that make people think that you're being racist and targeting only the anti-aliens? Specisist? Whatever?"

"I had thought that," he said. "But, if we make the prison for everyone, including non-humans, then we run the risk of them either corrupting others into joining their cause, or they'll kill whoever the non-humans are that get put in there."

I thought about it for a second and finally agreed

with him. "You have a point. But, if you can't do that, then what are the..." I never finished my sentence. I tripped over something on the ground, and in an attempt to not look totally inept, I tucked myself into a ball and rolled into the wall.

I placed my hand on the wall and used it to push myself up to my feet. Takar was looking at me, and opened his mouth to say something when the wall started to move. I jumped away from it, turning in the air to see what was going on.

The wall rose, revealing a... "Ho—ly SHIT!"

I was looking at a giant eye that stood as tall as me.

An eye. No question.

It was, massive green with a golden brown circle surrounding a black iris.

One, massive, eye.

My mind stopped working as Takar grabbed me and pushed me behind him.

The only thought running through my head was "We found it!"

But now what?

TAKAR

I instinctively grabbed Daphne and shoved her behind me. Whatever this was, I was not going to let it get to her without doing everything I could to stop it first.

Maybe those skrelling vines would help her. I could only hope.

Daphne clutched onto my arm tightly, but I didn't get the sense that it was from fear.

A quick glance down at her confirmed my suspicions. She was excited.

Of course, she was.

The wide-eyed glee on her face was unmistakable.

"What is it?" I asked.

"It's him," she whispered in awe. She looked up at me and smiled. "It's him," she repeated. She stepped around me and approached the eye, stopping only a foot or two short of touching it.

It blinked, slowly, as if it was studying her as much as she was studying it. Suddenly, the ground began to shake beneath us. Daphne fell to a knee as I reached for her, pulling her close. I tried to keep us steady as the ground continued to shake and move.

Vines came out of the ground, breaking the dirt floor away, covering us in dirt and dust. The vines began to weave themselves together into two strands and lay themselves flat against the wall, as if they outlined a pathway for us to follow.

We looked at one another, then at the path. "Do we follow it?" Daphne asked. This was the first time that she seemed nervous, apprehensive about this.

I looked down and gave her a reassuring smile. "Why not?" I asked rhetorically. "You've come this far, dragging me along with you. Are you saying that I have to drag you along now?"

She cocked her head to the side, and pursed her lips at me. "You're not going to stop me?"

I shrugged. "Why bother? It's time to figure this all out," I answered.

She smiled, grabbed my hand, and pulled me behind her. I was walking with her after only two steps, unconsciously slowing down my pace so I didn't force her to move faster than necessary.

We followed the path that the vines created. They led us through a series of tunnels, different in appearance from the ones we had been exploring. These were rougher, as if they were created either in haste or simply hadn't been rubbed smooth yet.

Those tunnels took us past some minor drop-offs, across some small crevices, and over some minor fissures in the ground. But the vines marked the way, helping and guarding us from danger. Wherever there wasn't a vine bridge to cross, there was an earth bridge. Some of them crumbled slightly under our weight, but they held as we crossed.

Only once did Daphne slip on one of the bridges, but I managed to snake my arm out to catch her, along with some help from three vines that had quickly braided themselves into a rope around her waist.

It was obvious that whatever was going on, we were safe.

Relatively.

We continued walking down more tunnels and across more bridges. Every few tunnels, the slope was definitively pointed downwards.

"We've been walking forever," Daphne said. "I can't tell if we're getting deeper or not. I've lost all sense of everything down here."

I had to agree with her. There was no sense of direction anymore, or time. I no longer knew how long we had been below ground, or even how long it had been since I'd woken up from that amazing dream.

"What are you thinking?" I asked her.

"I don't know," she said with a shake of her head. "Do you think we should turn back?"

"Are you getting cold feet?"

"Well...I don't know," she said. "I just...when we saw the eye, I got really excited. I was thinking that we were going to find the center of this thing, and all we've done is just walk for a really long time and we've found nothing. It's...it's discouraging, you know?"

I nodded. As I opened my mouth to respond, the wall to my left started shaking and rumbling, bringing dust down on our heads. Within a few seconds, the wall broke away, revealing another cavern.

And the vines path led straight into it.

When the dust cleared, the awe that I felt at the sight of the previous cavern was nonexistent when compared to the amazement I felt here.

This cavern dwarfed the first one by nearly twenty times the size. Foliage that was much bigger than the previous cavern filled the space.

Colors that I had never seen before were in the previous cavern...in this cavern were so many shades and colors that I didn't think the universe knew of them. There was a forest-like area in the far left corner, a field of yellow man-sized flowers below our feet, ponds, streams, and waterfalls filling the cavern with moisture and sound as they fed the plant-life.

Daphne began slapping my arm with both of her hands, her slaps becoming more rapid and more violent as she tried to get my attention. When I looked down to see why she was slapping me, she pointed straight ahead.

In front of us was...if this thing wasn't a plant, it certainly looked like one. Suspended from the ceiling was a massive creature with a flower-bud like head. Vines stretched out from the creature all the way to the ceiling and the walls to my left and right and, as I moved to see past him, I could see vines stretched out behind him as well.

Great, now I'm changing pronouns from 'it' to 'him,' I thought as I tried to drink in the magnificence of what it was.

What he was.

When we had first seen the eye, it was as tall as Daphne. Overwhelming all on its own.

Now, seeing the rest of the body attached to that five-foot-something eyeball...I felt as little as an ant.

He was a giant green figure with what looked like petals of intense blues, reds, yellows, whites, and mixtures of each making up the flower-bud head. He didn't carry a humanoid shape, but I had the feeling that if he wanted to, he could walk the face of the planet in a matter of minutes if he chose to.

No one had ever accused me of being fanciful before.

I didn't think I was being so now.

The sheer size of him…I could see why this cavern needed to be so much larger than the last one. I could see how it was able to create and control vines that could encompass a city.

"This. Is. Amazing," Daphne whispered as she held my arm.

I had no words. To try to take all of this in, I needed every conceivable brain cell, and answering her statement took too much work. My brain was incapable of fully accepting what I was seeing.

Daphne started to sit down on the ledge, dangling her feet below her. "Sit down with me," she said, patting the spot next to her. "I think I need a moment to take all of this in."

I carefully sat down, not wanting my weight to make the ledge break. The ground ended, a short ledge sticking out over the floor of the cavern several hundred feet below us. To our right, far below on the cavern floor, was one of the lakes, so clear that I could see the fish swimming in it and the plant life swaying in it. I had a sudden vision of myself diving into the lake and enjoying the cool waters. It was such an attractive vision that I started to lean forward on the ledge.

I pulled myself back and looked at Daphne. I don't think I had ever seen her, or anyone else, smile so genuinely, or so hugely. I felt my own face crease into a smile. "So?" I asked.

"What?"

"Is it what you were looking for?" I asked.

She nodded and looked back at the cavern. "Oh, my, yes. It's so incredible," she answered breathlessly. "This is beyond my wildest imagination. Did you ever think something could have been more beautiful than the last cavern?" Her eyes searched mine and they sparkled with joy.

You, I thought.

Instead, I shook my head. "No. I thought the last cavern was the most beautiful place I had ever seen... and considering I've been to a few planets, that's saying something...but this," I swept my arm out to attempt to encompass the totality of this cavern. "This is, as you said, beyond imagination."

"I've never thought that I could ever find a treasure such as this," she breathed out as she lay her head against my arm.

I moved, then wrapped my arm around her and cradled her to me. "Neither did I," I whispered back.

We sat there for several long minutes, drinking in

the scene before, below, and above us. I felt…what did I feel? I felt comfortable. That was it, I felt comfortable sitting here with her cradled under my arm.

Suddenly, I felt her start to shake. I looked at her in concern to see that she was laughing.

"What's so funny?" I asked.

She looked up at me and took in a deep breath to calm herself. "I just realized, my little hand-held scanner isn't going to be nearly big enough to scan him." She jutted out her chin in the direction of the Puppet Master.

"Hmm," I hummed. "I think you have a good point. Then again, I don't think we have anything *anywhere* big enough to scan him properly."

She started laughing again. This time I joined her. It felt good to just relax and let loose a little, and that was exactly what I was currently doing. Even if I had wanted to do something to the Puppet Master, after seeing this and the sheer enormity of what he was…I wouldn't even make a leaf move on him.

"So, what now?" she asked, her hand lightly caressing my arm.

"I have no idea," I answered.

"Perhaps I can answer that question," came a voice. Both of us were startled.

"Did you hear that?" Daphne asked.

I nodded. "Yes. Did it sound like it was in your head?"

She nodded.

"Good. Just wanted to make sure I wasn't losing my sanity," I said.

"Trust me, my young friends. You are most certainly not losing your sanity." We looked at one another, then at the creature suspended in the middle of the cavern. *"I believe that it is time we speak."*

DAPHNE

I clutched Takar's arm, certain that if he weren't holding me up, I would've toppled right over the edge of the ledge.

"Stop leaning forward," Takar chuckled. He forced me to my feet and to take a step away from the ledge.

"I didn't realize I was." I couldn't take my eyes off the creature...the Puppet Master. A frown pulled at the corner of my mouth. Such a sinister name for something that didn't seem to be sinister at all.

"I am not sinister, as your species says," the voice came again.

Such a strange, lovely voice that sounded like a thousand different voices blended into one. High and sweet, but somehow also deep and melodic.

My head started to ache as I attempted to pull apart

the different sounds into something that made sense to me. I quickly gave up.

"I have so many questions," I murmured.

"I have many answers," the Puppet Master replied.

"How smart are you?" I blurted and immediately felt embarrassed. I would've liked to ask a more intelligent, sophisticated question. Then again, I didn't wake up this morning thinking that I'd be talking to a giant plant.

"I have the wisdom of countless eons," the Puppet Master replied.

"Are you technically a plant?" I asked.

"I am not a plant as you define it. But I am not an animal. Your kind has never encountered me. There is no word in your language to describe what I am."

"What are you, if you're not a plant?" I tilted my head to one side. I heard Takar laugh softly behind me. "What?" I looked back over my shoulder at him.

"I am," The Puppet Master replied. *"I was created from the cosmic dust of the universe's growth. I have traveled through untold galaxies and multiple dimensions. I exist with understanding that would bring you to tears. I sleep as countless civilizations rise, peak, fall, and die. For me it is but the passage of a breath."*

"I always think you can't get more curious and, somehow, I'm always surprised," he replied. His smile was sweet and dreamy. I felt myself melt a little.

"I'm going to take that as a compliment," I grinned.

"You should," Takar confirmed. "Now, go back to asking your questions."

"You can ask one, if you want," I offered, realizing I was hogging the Puppet Master.

"I'm sure you'll ask any question I might have," Takar assured me. With a nod, I turned back to the Puppet Master. Though it didn't have a face, per se, I could still *see* a patient expression in its form.

"Um," I fumbled with my words. "How old are you?"

"I am older than your Skotan companion's sun, my friend," The Puppet Master answered as I momentarily gasped. *"I can see in my memories the formation of the planet your ancestors knew as Earth. For me it was but a moment ago."*

"Right," I nodded definitively. "What connection do you have to the planet?"

"I will try my best to help you understand."

I nodded and waited for the Puppet Master to continue. I reached for Takar's hand and gave it a squeeze, partially out of fear but mostly out of excitement.

"I am the force that grows this planet," the Puppet Master explained. *"I send my lifeforce out into your world. Every plant, flower, and shred of grass is connected to my lifeforce. The planet grows around me as hair or skin grows on your body."*

"That's impossible," I breathed. I needed to update my definition of impossible. I was less than an ant to this creature.

"Let me show you, it may aid your understanding." The Puppet Master lifted a willowy thin vine so that it hovered in front of my face. My first reaction was to step back. Takar caught my shoulders as I nearly stepped on his foot.

The hovering vine paused. The Puppet Master waited for me to step forward. The vine tapped lightly between my eyes. I saw a large, dark sphere. Then, something beneath the surface lit up bright white. It was the shape of the Puppet Master and its vines. The light branched out until huge sections of the dark sphere were glowing white. I recognized those areas as the expansive forests and the swamplands of the planet.

"That's all from you?" I asked.

"That's correct," the Puppet Master confirmed.

"What about the sentient plants? And all the creatures?" I asked.

"When I was young, I didn't know how to fully contain my power. Those creatures were the result. I'm still quite fond of them," the Puppet Master sounded like it was laughing. I found myself smiling.

"You were young once?" I asked.

"Of course, aren't we all? My lifespan may be longer than yours, but we experience the same stages of life."

"Does that mean you'll grow old and die one day?" I asked.

"*One day,*" the Puppet Master confirmed. "*Though I am still young compared to the others.*"

I felt Takar perk up in interest.

"There are others?" He asked.

"*Yes,*" the Puppet Master said.

"How many? Where are they? Do you talk to them?" I asked my questions in rapid fire.

"*I do not know our precise numbers. There were more, not far from here, but they have recently gone silent. It is concerning,*" the Puppet Master replied.

"What do you mean, silent?" I pressed.

"*Just that. Communication between myself and the others of my kind is not a frequent occurrence. We aren't a social species. We communicate every few centuries as a way to judge our numbers. A few didn't answer last time.*"

"How long ago was that?"

"*Several thousand years by how humans measure time,*" the Puppet Master. I frowned.

"What do you think happened?" Takar asked.

"*There was a disturbance in deep space. Subtle. I doubt your mechanisms and devices would've picked up on it. I've never felt the likes of it before.*" I didn't think my interest could be more piqued, yet it was. "*There were rumors of an ancient enemy that had awoken. An enemy that was seeking to sway the lesser races. An enemy that thrived on chaos where my kind thrived on life."*

"You think there's something else out there?" I asked.

"There are things in this universe that even I don't know about. The universe and all of its secrets are more than you can fathom. There are forces so malevolent that you will pale in fear for the rest of your short, simple lives. There are similar forces for good and order that will protect you."

"Believe me, I'm beginning to learn that," I joked. I'd only recently learned that humans weren't the only intelligent species. In fact, humans seemed near the bottom of the chain in terms of advancement.

I stole a glance at Takar. I wondered what he'd seen in his lifetime.

"If you know the exact location of the planets that went silent, maybe we could check on them for you," I offered. The Puppet Master paused, as if it was taking a breath.

"Your kind offer is touching. But I do not know the location of my silent siblings in terms that your sensors and scanners would understand." There was a melancholy note in the voice in my mind.

"Could it have been the Xathi?" I asked Takar. "They haven't been to this corner of the universe before." I turned back to the Puppet Master. "Could that be it?"

"The Xathi are not the problem," the Puppet Master

said serenely. *"But they started the sequence of events that disrupted the delicate balance of this world. They are an abomination, but they are but a symptom. A sign of greater corruption in the universe that my kind has long sought to quell."*

"They have a bad habit of being evil," Takar said dryly. "Would you know if any Xathi still live on this planet?"

"What?" I looked up at Takar with wide eyes.

"There's always a chance of survivors," Takar said gently. "There could be a pocket group hiding out, licking their wounds." I gave an involuntary shudder.

"There are no Xathi here," the Puppet Master assured me. *"If there were, know that I would have wiped them out."*

"You're on our side, aren't you?" I asked.

"I am on the side that will ensure the survival of this planet, and thus the survival of myself, and the balance of the universe," the Puppet Master replied honestly.

"You're kind of like a heart," I mused. Takar gave me a puzzled look.

"A human heart?" There was humor in the Puppet Master's voice.

"Yes," I beamed. "You bring life to every part of my home."

"I suppose that's true," the Puppet Master said. *"In your limited understanding of the universe, it is the most apt comparison."*

"You know what that means?" I said to Takar.

"That you were right and I was wrong?" he sighed.

"No. Well, yes. That's not what I wanted to say. I wanted to say that if we want to get our planet back to where it needs to be, we need to work with it." I jerked my chin in the direction of the suspended flower bulb.

Takar gave me a skeptical look.

"Oh, come on!" I implored. "You can't possibly think that this creature wants to destroy us now."

"I don't," Takar clarified. "I'm just not sure how much we can do."

"I will provide guidance," the Puppet Master offered. *"We are simple creatures, though that may be hard for you to believe. Time has made us patient. The secrets of the universe have made us wary."*

"What species are you, anyway?" I asked.

"We have no formal name. We were here before the younger races, and never needed to name ourselves. When we roamed the stars at first, the universe was young. We were all alone."

"I'm sure you could've gotten a name if you wanted to," I replied. "But you kept yourself a secret from us this whole time."

"The last time I was awake, your races were not here," The Puppet Master explained. *"This world was in perfect balance."*

"I suppose we ruined that, didn't we?" I bit my bottom lip.

"The actions of your race were done to ensure survival. I cannot hold it against you."

"We should stop here," Takar said quickly.

"What's wrong?" I asked.

"General Rouhr should be here. Giving him a report is not enough. He needs to see this," Takar explained.

"Is that all right?" I asked the Puppet Master.

"We can't just invite people into his home without asking," I said to Takar.

"If it will help, any friend of yours is welcome here."

"They're all going to feel so foolish for thinking you were some kind of monster from a nightmare," I laughed.

"I hope I will not have to become a nightmare to preserve this world," the Puppet Master replied grimly. My smile dropped. *"Worry not. I am reasonable."*

Another vine rose up so that it appeared to be standing beside me. I reached out and gently touched the vine, feeling the life humming beneath my fingers.

TAKAR

"So, how do we get the general down here? Actually," I amended, "how do I get into contact with him, or anyone? My comm was lost in the fall, remember?"

"I have found what you speak of, my warrior friend," the Puppet Master's multilayered voice said in my mind. As it spoke, a vine slithered up from the bottom of the cavern. I watched as it rose higher and higher, stopping just in front of me, my comm unit balanced perfectly on a small bent portion.

I reached out and grabbed it. "Thank you," I said. "But, what about my first question? How do they get down here to see you and..." I waved my hand to indicate everything, "all of this?"

"I will ensure a pathway is prepared for them," he answered.

I nodded, apprehensively. Despite the conversation with him and his explanation of what he was, I was still worried. What if all of this was a trap of some sort, designed to bring us down here where we would be fighting it in its home, surrounded by thousands of vines and untold tons of dirt.

However, if he was telling us the truth, then the information and potential unity we could make with him would be beyond words. I shook my head and clicked on the comm unit. "Rokul?"

"Takar!" he shouted back at me. "What's been going on? Where have you been?"

I had to cut him off or he would never give me a chance to answer. "Rokul! Calm down. Take a breath," I ordered.

I was unsure if that worked, but when the comm came back on again, it was Sylor speaking to me. "Your brother has barely been able to keep himself together."

"I gathered," I responded. "How long has it been since our last communication?"

"At least ten hours," was the answer. Ten hours since we last talked to them. Ten hours? Had it really only been ten hours? That seemed nearly impossible. I could have sworn that I had counted out at least four hours of walking, and that would have meant that our time sleeping and my time fighting my near unconsciousness wasn't nearly as long as I had thought. "Have you discovered anything?"

His question brought me back to the present. "Yes," I answered. "But it's not something that I can describe. You need to get into contact with the general and have him come here. Anyone that he feels relevant should come as well."

"Are you not concerned about safety? Yours or theirs?" he asked. Even though it sounded as an accusation against my concern for gathering all of the leaders together, it was more of a question to ensure that I felt everything was safe enough.

"Safety is a concern, but the reward is well worth the risk," I answered.

That was apparently enough for him.

"Very well. It will take time, however. At the time of our departure, many members of the teams were dispersed to deal with the damage of the vines throughout the human settlements on this planet," he explained.

That was right. I had almost forgotten about that. It didn't matter. "I understand that, but make it happen, Sylor," I called back. "Believe me when I say it's imperative."

"Affirmative," Sylor called back. "We will come back into contact with you when we are back in range."

"Thank you, Sylor," I said. "Before you go, how's my brother?"

"You want to know how I am?" my brother's voice came on in the background. Suddenly, it was the dominant voice on the comm, as if he had turned his comm back on. "You disappear for ten hours, no word, no nothing. The last I heard was that woman croaking something about turning off the sonar scan, all while there was some weird noise in the background. Then nothing."

"We fell," I told him. "We fell and I lost my comm unit for a bit. But we found him, we found my comm, all is well and you need to get Rouhr and whoever else he deems necessary here."

"Who's 'him'?" my brother shot back.

"The Puppet Master," I answered. There was nothing on the comm after that for several moments. I chuckled to myself. I could just see my brother staring at the comm as if it had just come to life, all while Sylor was trying to get everyone to the transports to bring back the others.

"I'll stay here, then," Rokul said through the comm. "Until Sylor returns with the others."

"Impossible," I heard Sylor's voice through Rokul's comm. "We need all three transport units, and you're our third pilot. Trevor is the only one of the humans capable of piloting these models."

"Fine," Rokul growled. "We'll be back soon."

"I know you will," I responded. "Especially with the way you fly," I added, trying to perk him up a bit.

There was silence again. I assumed they left, Sylor certainly already on the transport comm, contacting the general.

"Do you mind if we wait to talk more until the general is here?" I asked the Puppet Master. "We really do want to speak more with you, understand more... but he's the right one. It shouldn't be a long wait."

A faint sense of amusement rolled through me. *"Time moves differently for you and me. I do not mind waiting."*

The giant eye shut.

I looked down at Daphne, who had been standing next to me the entire time. "What now?"

She shrugged. "I don't know. You don't have any ideas?"

I mimicked her shrug. "We could sit and talk," I suggested.

"About what?" she asked as she sat back down on the ledge.

I joined her. "Everything we've discovered down here," I said aloud. *That dream I had,* I thought quietly.

"Okay," she smiled, something that I had started off thinking was annoying, but now thought that it was beyond beautiful. "Can you believe this?" she asked.

"Everything that I argued for and against are right and wrong at the same time."

I nodded. "It seems to be that way. He looks so much like a plant that you can't help but consider him as one. Include in that the control he has of the vines and, if you can believe his claims, the fact that he brings life to the foliage above…it certainly seems as though he's a very complex plant."

"Yeah, but then if you think about his obvious intelligence, his ability to generate his own body heat, and the fact that he doesn't need the sun for photosynthesis, it all point to some sort of non-plant organism," she said, her voice low but filled with glee.

We continued speaking for a bit longer about everything we thought, but it was essentially the two of us merely repeating ourselves with all the same points from the tunnels, except now I was less suspicious and concerned with the danger.

Eventually, we stopped talking and just looked out at the cavern. The sight still took my breath away. Besides the lack of natural light…the cavern was lit by the same bioluminescence that had been present in the other cavern, as well as some glowing crystals…the other thing that caught my attention was that there were no animals down here. It was strictly the vegetation and the water.

Okay, there were the fish swimming in the water,

but I didn't see anything else. Either the animals were all experts at remaining unseen, or there simply weren't any outside the water. I began to imagine what it would feel like having a house down by the water, then my imagination placed that same home next to an above-ground lake or sea. The prospect of living underground certainly didn't seem to work for me.

"Can I tell you something?" Daphne asked, breaking me from my daydreams.

"Of course," I answered back, looking down at her and seeing a bit of worried hesitation in her eyes. "You can tell me anything," I added.

She smiled shyly as she looked back out at the cavern, her legs swinging out over the ledge. "I…well, I, uh…I had a dream about us."

I stiffened a little as she said that. Did she have the same dream as I'd had?

"I dreamt that we were together, like…*together* together. We had two kids, a house, and a life together," she explained.

I nodded, wanting to know what else she was going to tell me about the dream. "Tell me about the dream," I whispered.

"Well, we were in bed, trying to sleep in, but couldn't because the kids were awake, trying to be quiet." She smiled a bit sheepishly as she gave me a sidelong glance. "We snuck in a bit of lovemaking under the covers and just barely finished before the kids attacked us and we all started tickling one another."

"How did this dream make you feel?" My heart was pounding. I had a lump in my throat and my stomach was currently doing its best to do as many somersaults as possible. If she liked the dream, I would admit to her that I'd had the same. If she didn't, I wasn't sure what I was going to do.

"It," she started, then hesitated as she looked up at me. Her eyes shone. "It felt real…and really, really good."

"It did?" I asked.

She nodded. "Mm-hmm."

"Then I must confess to you," I said as I grabbed her hand. "I had the same dream. A little boy and a little girl with skin the same as yours and hair the same as mine."

Her eyes went wide as I spoke.

"I really liked the dream, as well," I said.

We stared at one another for several moments, her hands caressing my own hand. Her hands were so small compared to mine. I liked that.

"Do you think that the Puppet Master had something to do with it?" she suddenly asked. "I mean, the fact that we both had the same dream?"

"I don't know," I said. "I hadn't thought of that." I truly hadn't. It was slightly unnerving to think that somehow, he had either influenced our shared dream, or had found a way for us to share the dream, meaning he was in our heads.

"Did you maybe want to…" she started, her cheeks turning red as she lowered one hand to my leg and ran it up and down my thigh.

In answer, I put my hand on her cheek and pulled her in for a deep kiss. As we kissed, her hand made its way up between my legs, grabbing my fully engorged member through my pants.

I ran my hand down from her cheek to her neck, to the curve of her shoulder, and then began massaging her breasts. I felt her hand unfastening my pants, releasing the building pressure of the fabric holding me in.

While her lips never left mine, I could feel her gasp as she grabbed my freed cock and realized that she was barely able to get a full grasp of it.

She pulled away from me, looked down, then looked back up at me, her eyes wider than I could believe possible.

"Maybe we should move away from the edge of the ledge," she breathed as she was stroking me.

I nodded, struggling to maintain my concentration. We stood up, Daphne never releasing me, and walked away down the tunnel. I finally stopped and went to reach for her, but she had already dropped to her knees.

I watched her lick her gorgeous lips and my breath hitched in my throat.

She pressed her mouth to the head of my cock first, teasing me with the warmth of her mouth, the firmness of her lips.

The sensation of that moment forced my eyes closed as I began to gently thrust against her. If this was how life with her was going to feel, I was gladly willing to spend it with her.

Her fingers trailed my abs, the points of her delicate nails and their light sensation making me less in control than I would normally admit.

That was okay with Daphne.

She traced around my navel and then slowly stuck that finger into her mouth, her eyes never leaving mine.

I panted. I wasn't going to beg, because I knew she would give me what I wanted. I could wait.

Probably.

Her wet finger replaced her lips, but not before she pressed another light kiss to the twitching head of my cock.

She stroked it, wrapping her soft hands over my length. She alternated soft to hard strokes, then brought her mouth back.

Lips closing over the tip, her hands stroked vigorously as her mouth closed over and stroked my shaft perfectly.

The light noises of her mouth as she bobbed up and down the head of my cock, the feel of her fingers wrapping around my balls, her darkening eyes fixed on mine.

It was too much.

"Your turn," I said roughly as I pulled from her, kneeling down until we were almost face to face.

"But I thought…." she murmured, voice drowsy with need as I slowly, carefully undressed her.

"I have to taste you," I insisted, voice still unsteady. "Right now."

Lifting her up, I pulled her on top of me, lining her pussy up over my mouth. I hovered her there for a moment, positioned my thumb to stroke her sensitive bud, and then my tongue feasted on her wet folds.

Daphne thrashed, the pleasure now erupting from her body. Her control was no match for my relentless pursuit of her pleasure. Unbelievably, my cock grew even harder as I listened to the sounds of her moaning.

Untethered to reality. Unbound by reason.

Her body was mine to have, to hold, and to exact every drop of desire from. Her honey tasted perfect, every drop of her arousal painting my lips and tasting like everything I'd ever wanted in the world.

For every sound of orgasm building within her, I increased my intensity, until she exploded around me, coming undone in my arms. I heard a sexy giggle from her lips as I knew she was orgasming, hard, and that wonderfully lightheaded sensation she'd just given me overtook her.

I wanted to please her forever.

It was the most important mission I could ever have.

DAPHNE

"Well, now," I whispered as I tried to catch my breath as I lay on top of him. I looked him in the eye as I smiled. "That was fun."

"That it was," he whispered back, running his hand through my hair. "I don't think I've ever enjoyed anything so much." He pulled me down and kissed me, the taste of my own arousal on his lips an intoxicating blend. There wasn't a single cell in my body that wanted to resist that kiss. As a matter of fact, every cell in my body wanted to do what we'd just done again. He made me feel more like a woman than I ever had in my life.

"You younger races focus too much of your time upon procreation. It's a wonder you get anything accomplished at

all," Puppet Master said, a hint of humor playing through our minds as he spoke.

"Yeah, well," I snapped back playfully, "when you have someone as gorgeous as this man here, it's hard to concentrate on much." I followed up my little statement with a playful nibble of Takar's nipples. Ooh, speaking of hard.

"You may wish to restrain yourselves. Your friends shall be here soon."

With a frown and a groan of disappointment, I pulled away from Takar…sort of. "What do you mean?" In answer, Takar's comm unit started beeping. We looked at one another, eyes wide.

"Guess we know what he meant," Takar said, reaching for his comm. "Takar here."

"Takar, this is General Rouhr. We will be arriving momentarily," the voice on the other side came back.

"Very well, sir," he responded, flashing me a smile. "Let me know when you land, and the Puppet Master will show you where to go."

"About that," came the gruff voice. "We're using the rift as soon as your brother returns with Tella."

Takar's face went pale, if someone with red skin could suddenly go pale. "We need to get dressed, now!" he whispered urgently. As we untangled ourselves and started getting dressed, he clicked the button on his comm to answer his boss.

"Sir, we were unable to use the rift to leave the vine dome." Takar looked around at the cavern, the walls writhing with extensions of our new friend. "The situation here is a bit more extreme."

"Try not to underestimate me, soldier," the voice answered. "Fen was able to pinpoint your location based on a combination of data on your previous comm and the sonic mapping done by your team. We will be arriving in the tunnels right above you."

Takar gulped. "That may be a bit of a problem, sir. There's not a lot of room right where we are currently standing. How many people are coming?"

There were a few seconds of pause, then the gruff voice I presumed belonged to General Rouhr came back on. "Nine."

Takar's eyes, somehow, unbelievably, got wider. "Um," he mumbled as he started looking around, spinning around a few times to try to figure out the spacing. "With us, that makes eleven. There's not enough room for eleven people, sir."

"I shall create a platform large enough and stable enough for all of you to stand or sit, as you please," the Puppet Master's voice echoed.

"Check that…according to the Puppet Master, there will be enough room for us all," Takar amended.

"Good," Rouhr said firmly through the comm. "Because we're coming through now." Takar and I quickly straightened up our clothes and ran our fingers through our hair.

I had no idea what the rift was, but from Takar's reaction, I figured that it was something I was going to witness in just a few seconds.

Bigger than shit, a few feet away from me, a colorful hole in the middle of the air opened, forcing Takar to scramble a few steps back, taking him farther away from me. The hole—maybe it was a tear—was rich and vibrant in its colors of yellow, orange, red, black, and white.

Stepping through the hole first was a large man that looked so much like Takar, I knew instantly that they were brothers. Behind him came a guy whose dark gray skin was covered in green circuitry-looking lines and another guy with green skin and purple...stripes everywhere. The Valorni and K'ver were both smaller than Takar and his brother, and each gave me the same nod that the brother had given me as they stepped through.

Number four through the rift was Annie, a look of consternation mixed with disappointment and anger on her face.

Heck.

"Hi, Annie," I said with a big wave and even bigger smile. She didn't buy it and continued to scowl at me as three more women walked through. I recognized Vidia, and had seen the other two in the same labs as Annie, but didn't know their names.

The second to last through the rift was a very grumpy-looking Valorni whose expression darkened when he looked at me, but filled with love when he looked at Annie. That had to be Karzin.

That meant that the last one through was the general. He had red skin, a bit faded, but red. He was covered with scars and looked to be older than everyone. He gave me a perfunctory look, then turned around as the rift vanished.

Takar stood there, at attention, already giving the general a salute. "Sir," he said.

"Easy, Takar," the general responded. "So, where is the Puppet Master?"

Takar pointed. As everyone turned to look, the collective gasp was mixed with a few 'oohs,' 'aahs,' and 'skrells.'

I tried my best not to smile.

When no one spoke for a few moments, I stepped forward. "Puppet Master, I think the easiest way to begin this whole proceeding is to show them what you showed us."

"Wait, what do you mean sh…" Karzin started to ask. Then he jumped and started looking around, but his eyes looked distant. Takar grabbed him to hold him still.

Within minutes, everyone started to either shake their heads or rub their eyes. "Holy hell," one of the women said.

Vidia looked over at her and gave her a motherly smile. "Yes, that was certainly different, Tella."

Everyone began to speak at the same time, four different conversations between ten different people as I stood and watched. This was pure insanity.

"I understand your confusion," Puppet Master said, causing every single one of the newcomers to virtually jump out of their skins. When the silence lasted longer than four seconds, I spoke up.

"That would be him," I explained.

"I apologize for startling you," Puppet Master said. *"And as I was saying, I understand your confusion. What I have shown you is something that is natural for my kind. Throughout the course of time, my kind has numbered in the thousands and have travelled to corners of the universe that none of your races have even conceived of existing.*

"I am, to use your parlance, the heart and life of this planet. I am what makes this planet live, and what returns this planet to normalcy when life tries to make a change."

"When you say 'change'," General Rouhr cut in, "am I to assume to mean us?"

"You assume correctly, Rouhr, General of the Vengeance *and leader of non-human forces,"* came the answer. *"The battle that you brought to this planet, whether*

you meant to or not, has upset the delicate balance of what I have created."

"How do we fix that balance?" Vidia asked.

"Before you answer that," the woman I didn't know interrupted. "What caused the imbalance? If we knew what it was, maybe we could help fix it."

"The enemy that you brought with you, the Xathi," Puppet Master started to answer. *"They are the imbalance. When their vessel crashed down upon the surface, there were several foreign pollutants that leaked into the ground, and therefore into me. Before my system was able to develop a counter to these pollutants to purge them from my body, they transferred to many portions of life above."*

"The plants that are dying, they're dying because of Xathi chemicals?" Annie asked.

"Correct," was the answer. *"The 'chemicals' that leaked have become a plague upon my creations. A plague that I am attempting to rectify."*

"I can understand your desire to repair yourself and your creation," Rouhr said. "But why attack the human settlements? They weren't the ones that caused the chemicals to seep into the ground."

"That is true. However, the materials that were being used by not only the humans, but by your kind, are needed to restore the balance of life. I can only create so much, and by you reaping the materials for your own use, I am unable to restore the life above."

With a heavy nod, Rouhr looked around at all of us. He turned back to the Puppet Master. "So, in our attempts to repair the damage that we inadvertently caused in our war with the Xathi, we were causing more damage."

"I regretfully say that you were. I did not intend to harm anyone. When I awoke, I was confused, angered. I merely intended to stop you on the surface from taking what was needed to restore the balance. In time, as the balance is restored, you are welcome to my bounty. But not before."

"What happens if you can't restore the balance?" the one Vidia had called Tella asked. Rouhr looked at her, a bit irritated I thought, then looked back at the Puppet Master.

"If I am unable to restore the balance of the planet that has grown around me, it will die and I will be forced to move on, as I have done countless times."

"Whoa, wait," Tella stepped forward, ignoring Rouhr's attempts to hold her back. "What the hell do you mean 'die'? If the planet dies, we all die with it."

"That is correct."

"Shit."

TAKAR

I watched and listened as Rouhr and the Puppet Master spoke. I began to wonder if the Puppet Master's voice truly was resonating in my mind or if it just sounded that way. I thought about the possibilities of what it would be like to be able to speak directly into a person's mind.

Let's see, I thought as they continued on with their conversation. *If I had the ability to speak into someone's mind, it would cut down on conversation time, as well as allow us to keep the conversation entirely private, unless one of us spoke about it openly later. That's not bad. But...if I was able to connect to someone's mind in order to speak to them directly, would that mean I could read their mind? If I could, would I want to? Would I be able to control what I heard from their mind or would I hear everything?*

You would hear everything in their mind, the Puppet Master's voice said, louder and clearer than before. The more unusual thing was that I still heard him speaking with Rouhr. *That's right, I can carry on several conversations at the same time. In answer to your inquiry, you would hear the thoughts of the person you were connected to. However, if there was too much emotion mixed in with those thoughts, they would be blocked.*

That means you've heard my thoughts the entire time I've been down here? I asked him in my head.

Not the entire time, but yes. I understand your distrust of me. I had the same distrust for you.

What changed your mind? I asked.

An image of Daphne touching the vines popped into my head. *I trust her, as do you.*

I had no counter to that. I did trust her. I liked her. If what we had done before the others arrived weren't proof of that, the fantasies I was currently having about her certainly were.

Why trust me? I asked him.

Because you trust her, he answered. *She is special, the first of your kind that was willing to try to speak to me and treat me as a living being, not simply an enemy. You followed her, tried to protect her, and listened to her. Despite your conscious thoughts of her, your subconscious trust of her was identical to that for your brother. Even though you questioned her, you allowed yourself to be swayed by her. That meant that you trusted her, even if you didn't realize it.*

I nodded. It made sense. I must have trusted her somehow if I was willing to let her drag me farther and farther down underground. Perhaps, and now that I thought about it, I found it sounding true in my mind, I had always wanted to find exactly this…the Puppet Master himself and the knowledge that he wasn't the enemy we had originally believed him to be. I hadn't really wanted him to be like the Xathi, just something that we needed to destroy.

"Dr. March," Rouhr started. "While I may not approve of your methods, I appreciate your," he posted, looking for the right word. "initiative in starting discussions with our new ally."

I grinned until his stern gaze fell on me.

"Takar." I straightened quickly. "You did well," he said. "Thank you for making the right decision here."

I nodded and gave him a salute. "It was my pleasure, general." Daphne and Rokul both looked at me with pride. Karzin nodded, Iq'her gave me an upwards turned thumb—something he had picked up from Stasia and the human children of Nyheim—while the women all nodded, or smiled, or—in Tella's case—softened their scowl.

Then Tella laughed, smacked me in the arm, and

said, "Good job, Stuffy," her nickname for me since I was always distant from them.

"Thank you," I smiled as I put my arm around her. Her eyes went wide in surprise, as did Rokul's. I gave her a slightly more than gentle squeeze. "Glad to hear you approve." I could have resorted to banter with her, like I did with my brother when we were alone, but this was more fun.

I should try the unexpected more often.

She was obviously surprised, and a bit at a loss for words.

I winked at my brother, flashed a smile at Daphne, and gave Tella one last squeeze as Rouhr finished speaking with Karzin, Vidia, and the Puppet Master. He turned to look at everyone. "Time to go home and begin working on the changes needed to fix the planet," he said. He got into contact with Fen and requested a rift back to Nyheim.

The portal opened and Daphne stared at it as the rest of the party walked through, one or two at a time.

"It's okay," I told her as I reached for her hand. She took it, her eyes never leaving the rift. "It's a little cold, and very disorienting the first time through," I explained. "But if you just never let go of me and walk through quickly, everything will be fine."

She nodded, her grip tight on my hand. As we walked forward, she hesitated slightly, but she pushed through. We entered the rift and everything in the universe twisted and became distorted. I took two steps through the inside of the rift before stepping out of it and back onto the streets of Nyheim.

Daphne was shivering next to me. Everyone gave her a quick empathetic smile...the first one or two times through the rift always messed with someone, but it eventually became simple. I had asked my brother and Tella what they felt, or saw, when they went through the rift. Each gave me a different answer, except for the cold part. It was absolutely freezing for that moment you passed through, but it was only for that moment.

"You okay?" I asked Daphne as I drew her in close.

She nodded vigorously. "You guys do that all the time?" she asked, her voice still shaking a bit.

"That we do, young lady," Rouhr answered. He turned his attention to me. "Report, on my desk, soon. Then get checked out by Evie, then take the rest of the day off. That's an order," he said.

"Understood, sir," I said. I wasn't going to argue. As everyone turned to go about the rest of their business and discuss what had just happened, I stayed behind with Daphne, my brother, and Tella.

"So," Rokul started. "Mind introducing us?"

"Oh," I had completely forgotten to do so, at least

properly. "This is my brother Rokul. He might be older, but I'm definitely the better one."

"Hmmpf," he said as he reached out and shook Daphne's extended hand. "He likes to pretend."

"And this," I continued on, ignoring his jibe, "is our resident botanist, roommate, absolute pain-in-my-posterior, and my brother's lover, Tella."

All three looked at me in wonder as Daphne and Tella said hello and exchanged pleasantries.

"Are you alright?" Rokul asked me.

I shrugged. "We're all family now," I said. "No point in acting like I'm pretending to be Sylor all the time."

He laughed. "Okay."

"So, what happens now?" Daphne asked.

I turned to face her, leaned down, and kissed her on the lips. "I, unfortunately, have to go file reports. But, if you're willing, I'd love to have dinner with you tonight. My brother can tell you where we like to eat and how to get there if you don't already know."

"Okay," she smiled. "Just don't forget me, okay?"

"Never," I answered. I could see out of the corner of my eye the other two staring at me as if I had been replaced by someone foreign. I looked at Rokul. "Take care of her?"

"Like you had to ask."

Tella took Daphne by the arm and started walking her away, the two of them talking in quiet voices. Rokul stayed behind with me. As the ladies continued walking, they started laughing.

"Why am I suddenly scared?" Rokul asked.

I shrugged. "I don't know. Is it because the women in our lives are suddenly best friends?"

"Yep," he said with an overexaggerated nod. "Yeah, that's what scares me. Have fun with the paperwork," he said as he clapped me on the shoulder and started jogging after them.

THAT NIGHT, while sitting at dinner, Daphne and I got to talking about subjects that didn't involve our little adventure underground. I learned a little more about her family, quickly realized that her parents' hovercraft was still out in the desert, ordered one of the security crew to rift out there and retrieve it for her, and laughed at the stories she told me about her time in school. Apparently, while an incredibly intelligent woman, she had a bit of a wild streak in her.

As we walked through the park near the restaurant after dinner ended, I volunteered to walk her home.

She seemed to hesitate, then finally gave in to my persistent question of "Is everything okay?"

"I don't exactly have a permanent place to live," she told me. "When the Xathi ship landed, I ran and hid. I came back to find my little place destroyed. I stayed with my parents, and just when I was getting a new place, the dome happened. My house was one of the ones on the north side of town that was toppled."

That was…distressing to hear. "Where have you been staying?" I asked her.

"Usually I stay at the hospital," she answered, then quickly added, "It's okay. I'm not homeless. I just work all the time," she said when my eyes went wide in concern.

That wasn't going to be good enough. "Then you must stay with me until we can figure out a more permanent living situation for you."

She just smiled. I took that as a good sign. We returned to the apartment that I shared with Rokul and Tella. They weren't home, or they were already in bed. Either way, we still walked silently through the apartment to my room. I offered to sleep on the couch, but she asked for me to stay.

As we lay in bed, we began to kiss and touch one another, our hands roaming each other's bodies, giving each other pleasure. It just felt…natural. It wasn't long before she was asleep against me, her body heat making me both comfortable and drowsy.

I closed my eyes.

DAPHNE

By the time I woke, the sun was already filtering through the blinds.

I turned to the side, momentarily disoriented, and realized that I was in Takar's apartment. And not just in his apartment: I was in his bed. Smiling to myself, I snuggled up against him, my heart beating happily as I felt the warmth of his half-naked body. I remembered how it felt to kiss him last night, the way his hands roamed up and down my body...

"G'morning," he said as he opened his eyes lazily. "Did you sleep well?"

I didn't even reply. I just looked straight into his eyes, focused on the wild beating of my own heart, and then closed the distance between us and crushed my mouth against his.

He returned my kiss at once, parting my lips with the tip of his tongue, and we embraced each other eagerly. I felt him lay one hand on my face, his fingers gently resting against my cheek, and I realized just how much I wanted.

Or to be honest, how much I needed him.

His fingers fell from my cheek to the nape of my neck, and he then weaved them into my hair. "I'm so glad I met you," he whispered softly. "I'm so glad you're here...with me."

"That makes two of us," I breathed out, my lips returning to his. He savored my lips eagerly, his free hand wandering down the side of my body, and I felt desire overtake me. My whole body was on fire, and its heat seemed to concentrate itself right between my hips.

"I want you, Takar," I told him, kicking the sheets back and jumping on top of him. With my knees on either side of his thighs, straddling him, I dragged my teeth across my bottom lip as I felt his hardness straining against his underwear. Swaying my hips, I pressed down on his hard cock with my own wetness, and an electric shiver shot up my spine as I did.

"And I want you, Daphne," he said, both his hands now resting on my ass. He stroked one of them up my back then, sliding my borrowed nightshirt off me. He cupped both my breasts at once, his gaze focused on the way my nipples hardened under his touch.

"I never felt like this before," I admitted with a soft whisper, resting both my hands on his naked chest. I feel his heartbeat against the palm of my right hand, and I smile as I realized that our hearts were in complete sync, their rhythms the same. "And I need you to take me, Takar...I need you to *fuck* me."

"I thought you'd never say it," he growled, hooking his fingers in the elastic band of my thong and pulled it against my outer thigh. The fabric tore in half a second, but neither of us cared about it. Pushing myself off him, I then yanked his boxers down his legs and released his erection, my heart skipping a beat as his cock sprung free.

It was bigger than any I had seen before, a perfect match to his muscular body. Large and thick, I wasn't even sure if my body could handle it...but I was more than willing to experiment with it and see what would happen.

I was a scientist, after all...a very curious, very wet, scientist.

I took a moment to appreciate his naked body, growing even wetter with each second my gaze lingered on the contour of his muscles, and only then did I reach for his hard shaft. Gently, I wrapped my fingers as far around it as I could, relishing the way it throbbed against the palm of my hand, and started flicking my wrist, stroking him at an increasingly faster rhythm.

"That's so good," he whispered. "Not yet, though." He had a wicked twinkle in his eyes. "First, I want to taste you again."

Takar spread my thighs and nuzzled his nose against my sensitive folds, making my clit and my pussy ache with need. His mouth suctioned around my clit, then his tongue flicked it lightly. My body was falling into the heat of his desires when his tongue lashed out, winning against all reason and all thoughts.

His fingers and his tongue took over my body, making me whimper with raw need.

I moaned, the feeling of his mouth servicing my every desire rousing a heady mix of lust and love. I wanted to feel the way he made me feel all the time.

My orgasm welled up inside me, a tide crashing against reality, blanking the world in a veil of white. I opened my eyes and looked at him, gazing up at me as his wide tongue lapped up every last drop of my desire.

"Wow."

My body felt boneless for a moment and Takar pressed kisses up and down my thighs, shivering around him.

As soon as I regained my strength, I was ready to take him on. My mouth watered with need for him, ready to pay him back in kind for the incredible orgasm he'd given me.

"Now I'm getting started on you." Shifting my position, I reached for the tip of his cock with my tongue and lapped at it softly, the way he tasted making my head spin. It wasn't long before I was rolling my lips down the length of his cock, and I only stopped when I felt him pressed against the back of my throat. Resting both hands on the top of my head, he started guiding my movements and my rhythm grew exponentially. I bobbed my head back and forth, devouring his cock as if my life depended on it, and Takar's small groans of pleasure started filling the bedroom.

"Daphne," he groaned, his heavy shaft weighing down against my tongue. I could tell he was trying to stop me, but I was having none of it.

Not this time.

I just started running my lips up and down his cock even faster, enjoying every little spasm of his member, and then... "Skrell!" he hissed past gritted teeth, his milky seed exploding into my mouth. I held my position, allowing him to fill my mouth, and then looked up into his eyes.

He looked back at me, probably enjoying the way I looked with his hard member between my lips, and offered me a wild grin. Slowly, I slid his shaft out of my mouth and, without a moment's hesitation, swallowed it all. I wasn't sure what it was, but there was something about Takar that just made me want to be wild. I felt safe in his presence, free to experiment and to break all boundaries.

"You're incredible," he told me, two fingers under my chin as he pulled me toward him. I straddled him once more, ready to have him inside me and to ride him into oblivion, but he had other plans. Grabbing me by the waist, he rolled to the side and forced me to lie on my back, pinning me between his body and the mattress.

"I don't want you to say it," I teased him. "I want you to show me just how incredible you think I am."

"I can do that." He grinned, grabbing his cock with one hand and angling it down so that its tip pressed against my slick folds. Arching my back, I prepared myself for what was about to come and laced my legs around his waist, eager to have him inside me.

He used the full strength of his hips to thrust, the whole length of his cock sliding inside me in one single movement.

Oh.

He froze as I did, waiting, while all of my attention was on where we joined.

This was… this was…

Perfect.

"More," I whispered, as he slowly drew back and

pumped into me again. "Harder," I moaned, "harder!" The sensations spiraled through me, intensifying every time he drove deeper into me, until he was fully seated.

Tightening my legs around him like a vise, I begged him to thrust even harder, and I felt my body burn from the inside out as he ravaged me. There was something primal about the way he took over my body, almost as if he was no longer a rational being but a wild creature, one whose single purpose in life was to make me explode with pleasure.

And that's exactly what I did.

He kept on bucking, until my inner walls started tightening around him, each nerve ending inside my body coming alive at once. Fireworks exploded behind my shut eyelids and I felt as if my brain was turning to mush inside my skull. I had never experienced anything like this, and I couldn't help but want more of it.

"Now's my turn again," I grinned, both hands on his chest as I forced him to roll to the side. He let himself go willingly, and I found myself on top of him once more, his length never sliding out of my body as we rolled on the mattress. My eyes stayed fixed on his as I dug my fingernails into his chest, already swaying my hips at a frantic rhythm, hell bent on riding him until he exploded for the second time.

"You are so perfect, Daphne," he told me, his parted lips summoning mine. I leaned down to kiss him, and he bucked upward the moment our lips connected, forcing my hips down on him, controlling our pleasure. It didn't take long before my body was being dragged under another tidal wave of rapture, the way Takar's cock throbbed against my inner walls enough to create a chain reaction.

We came at the same time, the sound of his aching groans blending with my ecstatic moans, our voices bouncing off the walls and returning to us like the purest music I had ever heard. We remained like that for almost a minute, neither of us daring to move as we tried to catch our breath.

"This was incredible," I finally said as I rolled to the side, sprawling myself on top of the mattress.

"It was more than that," he whispered. "It was perfect."

"That's what being with you feels like...it feels perfect."

"I don't know how to say it, Daphne," he continued, propping himself up on one elbow, his eyes locked on mine, "but I feel I must say it all the same. You're special to me, and I've come to care for you. I can no longer imagine a life without you."

"Takar..."

"Remember when you asked me if I had a life outside of work? Well, now I do...and that's you." He made a short pause, almost as if to muster the necessary courage to continue, and only then did he say it. "I love you."

I held my breath for a second.

My heart did a somersault inside my chest.

A whirlwind of thoughts took over my mind. Was this just an after effect of our time with the Puppet Master? Stress-bonding from being lost together in the tunnels? Lingering emotions from the dream?

So many questions.

And for once, it didn't matter.

I had my answer.

"I love you, too, Takar."

TAKAR

After breakfast...or lunch...what was that meal called that the humans said came between breakfast and lunch? Brunch? Whatever it was, after we ate, Daphne went to go see her parents to let them know that she was safe and still alive. Afterwards, she told me, she would go to the hospital to check in there and get back to work.

I was sad that she had to leave, but it was the right thing. We couldn't just stay in the apartment in each other's arms for the rest of eternity, no matter how much either of us wanted to.

So, after she left, I showered, gathered my gear together, and went to find my brother. I found Rokul working his shift in the armory, going over everything and ensuring that things were how they were supposed to be. Today, he was double checking inventory.

The armory felt as close to home for many of us as our own dwellings did. More so for some, such as myself, my brother, and Axtin. Then again, lately Axtin had been spending less time at the armory. Rumor had it he and Leena were attempting to have children.

Apparently, the worries generated from Vrehx and Jeneva's pregnancy didn't extend to them, especially since Axtin was a Valorni. He didn't have the issue with the scales that we Skotan s did.

The inside of the armory was simple. The locked outer door could only be accessed by biometric, optic, and numerical code. There was a sensor installed on it by Zarik, one of our engineers, that also ran a quick biometric scan of you to ensure that you were allowed within the armory. If you were not, a small alarm went off to remind you that you needed to get signed in by one of the commanders. If the alarm was not turned off within a certain amount of time, an alert was sent out to each member of the security team, each strike team, and all the leaders.

He had gone a bit overboard, but I liked it. Inside, there was a counter that had been made part of the cage that locked away all the weapons and ammunition, another door identical to the first connected to the counter. There was a small portion of the cage left open to have some of the smaller weapons passed through, but too small for a person to get through.

Inside the cage were three steel tables and six aisles. The tables were there for disassembly, cleaning, and reassembly purposes, as well as home to the four datapads used to inventory everything.

Ever since the battle with the Xathi ended, we had been able to restore our weapon and ammunition counts, as well as modify our own weapons. The humans had some weapons that we did not, and after studying them, Axtin and Sylor had been able to make several hybrid-style weapons.

Using the human technology and melding it with ours gave us new weapons, better weapons, and a better way to make ammunition. While we were still low on the ammunition we used for our bigger weapons, like Daxion's portable cannon, we had more than enough—hopefully—for the slightly smaller and modified weaponry.

Also, Axtin, Dax, Sylor, and Sakev had all managed to find the time to forge and create either newer versions of their personal weapons, or simply to duplicate them. Axtin had his original hammer, and her two 'little sisters' as he called them, in his own possession, but there were two more of the big hammers and six more of the little ones.

Dax had made four more crossbows, yet to his

frustration only managed one duplicate of his never-ending-quill. That was understandable, the technology needed to turn organic materials into his crossbow bolts was powerful, and difficult.

Sylor and Sakev had come together to make some new swords, each of them outfitted with a small electrical pack that not only cut or stabbed their opponent, but also electrocuted them at the same time.

It was an impressive array. I, however, had never been one to go that route. I was much more comfortable with my handguns, my rifle, and my collection of knives—something that had grown thanks to Rokul finding that kid out in that little no-name village where he and Tella had first met.

The knife he had gotten me was a personal favorite, and I had occasionally gone to work with the boy on my latest commissions...plural.

"Brother," I said as I found him in one of the back aisles of the armory.

He looked over, nodded, and returned to his counting of the ammo clips. I allowed him to finish before I spoke up again.

"How are things going?"

He smiled. "Nearly as good for me as they are for you." He turned to me, his smile becoming more mischievous.

"And what's that supposed to mean?" I asked,

absentmindedly taking one of the rifles down and setting it on the table.

"I haven't inventoried that yet," he said. He quickly scanned it, then moved back to inventorying the rest of that aisle. As he scanned and checked, he answered my question. "You did something that I didn't think you would do."

"What's that?" I asked as I pulled off the stock and began working on the rest of the disassembly.

"You found yourself someone that you want to be with, someone other than me that takes up your sense of responsibility," he said. I detected something in his voice that made me turn to look at him. He was looking at me with a look I hadn't seen on his face since our family was killed.

"What's the matter?" I asked, taking a step toward him.

He shook his head. "I'm sorry. I just..." he turned his head and let out a big breath of air. He turned back to me, a forced smile on his face. "You've taken care of me since as long as I can remember, which is saying something, because it was supposed to be my job to take care of you."

"It never bothered me, brother," I said.

"Still," he said, his face still sad. "You stepped up and cared for me, making sure that my impulsiveness didn't end up killing us and you didn't have to. You joined the military because of…"

"Because of the Xathi," I interrupted. "And even if they hadn't attacked, I was still heading in that direction."

He nodded. "I know, but you followed me. You were smart enough to go anywhere, to do anything in the fight with the Xathi, instead you followed me. You were there to keep me as much out of danger as you could."

"You would have done the same," I countered. This was not like him. "What's wrong with you?"

He threw up his arms in exasperation. "I'm trying to thank you and apologize for everything. I wasn't the most reliable brother around, and I…I sort of used you. I was so used to you always being there for me that I took you for granted. You are far too smart to be my damn babysitter," he exclaimed loudly. "I mean, look at what you've done when you haven't been busy taking care of me."

I was at a loss for words. I had never thought that he felt this way. "What are you trying to say, Rokul?"

"I'm saying that I'm proud of you."

I was blown away. The force with which he said those words were like nothing I had heard from him before.

"You are…without a doubt…the smartest person I have ever met," he continued. "It doesn't take you very long to learn something, and no matter who we're working with and what their specialty is, you end up understanding it within hours, a few days at the absolute most. I know that when you're not constantly looking after me, you can, and generally do, accomplish anything."

"Thank you," I said. "But, if you're about to say something stupid, like we should separate or something, I will beat you to the floor."

He grinned. "I'm not saying that at all, and you know you can't beat me in a fight."

"Well," I said slowly, playfully.

"Ha, ha. You're funny," he said, finally smiling. This was the brother that I knew. "Look, I'm just trying to say that I'm proud of you for finding someone to spend your life with."

"You think Daphne and I will spend our lives together?" I asked.

He nodded. "A giant multicolored flower told me."

Of course the Puppet Master had told my brother.

"That, and Daphne and Tella have become instant friends. She mentioned the dream," he explained. His expression became serious again. "You need to concentrate on *your* life now. I have my life, and someone to be with. You do, too, now. We will always be brothers, always inseparable, but we both have our own families now."

"Families?" I asked, a smile creeping onto my face.

He shook his head. "Not like that. I don't think I'm ready to become a father," he chuckled. "An uncle, yeah."

"Shut up."

He laughed. "But you get what I'm trying to say, right?"

I nodded. "We're family, all of us, but we sometimes have to be our own family." He nodded as I continued. "It might be nice to see how you grow. Besides, you've got a lot of catching up to do," I said with a grin.

Now it was his turn to look confused. "What do you mean?"

I smiled broadly. "Well, I've always been faster, stronger, smarter," I drew out each word just slightly to let him know I was joking, "better looking, and more interesting than you are."

It dawned on him finally. "Nice."

DAPHNE

Whenever I had the chance, I used Takar's spare comm unit to call this Fen person and have a rift opened so I could visit with Puppet Master. After the first few times, Fen set up an AI to respond to my voice and open a rift for me, since I was always going back to the same spot.

How brilliant must she be, to just build an AI to do a task for her?

I couldn't wait to meet her, but some things had to come first.

Takar had been right when he said that I would get used to traveling through the rift. Now I only felt a few heartbeats of vertigo each time.

Over the past few days, I had gone to visit the Puppet Master at least two or three times a day. Today's lunch called for another trip. I called Fen, asked for a rift, and stepped through when it popped up.

"It is good to see you once again, friend Daphne," his voice projected into my mind as I stepped through the rift and into a tunnel, where a chair of vines carried me down to his chamber.

"Hey there, PM," I said as I waved to him. I sat myself down at the ledge, noticing a small platform of vines sticking out a short distance underneath me. Guess my near fall yesterday prompted that.

There was no way I would survive a fall if that wasn't there.

"Your mate would never forgive me if I let something happen to you," he said, reading my mind. *"If you were injured or killed while in my care, he would bring a weapon that could harm me. I've read it in his mind. I would also miss our talks."*

"Then I better be more careful, huh?" I said as I scooted back a little. I set down my lunch bag and opened it, taking out my sandwich. PM moved a vine over by me, offering up a small selection of fruits. "Thank you," I said.

"It is my pleasure. What do you wish to speak about today?"

I took half a moment to finish chewing my first bite of my sandwich, then answered. "Well, I wanted to talk about the others out there like you."

"And what do you wish to know?" he asked, tilting his head to the side as he shifted slightly. I had already learned from him that every time he shifted, it was to open the buds that needed to be opened when the sun hit them. The level of concentration that was needed to monitor every single plant on the planet, it must have been insane. But the more I thought about it, the more I realized that almost everything he did must be done subconsciously, just like us.

As humans, our brains sent out millions of tiny little commands every second. We didn't have to think about making our heart pump to send blood flowing through our veins and arteries so our body parts could work. We didn't have to think about our liver cleansing our body, or our stomach processing the food we ate, breaking it down into the nutrients we needed to survive. It just happened.

Our brain did everything we needed it to do because it had to be done. It was just a natural process. The people that said that we only used ten percent of our brains were…well, they were off on their estimates. We actually used all of our brains, which was a no-brainer —pun!—but our conscious use of our brains ranged from five percent to fifteen percent…some as many as twenty percent. However, those that used twenty percent of their brains usually flamed out and died young.

They were geniuses, but they were eccentric…or had some other form of…abnormality, so they ended up dying young because they tended to forget to do something that the brain normally would have done on its own to protect itself and the body.

PM was doing the same thing. It was the only explanation that made sense to me.

"Very true, my friend. Many of my actions are done automatically without any conscious thought of my own. I have found," he said, *"that if I think about what I do instinctively, I make mistakes. Can I tell you a small secret?"*

"Please," I said, happy to hear any secrets PM was willing to share.

"The desert in which I first created the crater, where the Urai live in the remnants of the Aurora, *was a mistake. It was originally lush grasslands, but then I began thinking about what I was doing there, and I lost control,"* he confessed.

I was blown away. To think, a place as beautiful as the desert wasn't supposed to be one. Just…wow.

"Now, my friend," he said, *"what is it you wish to know about those like me?"* he asked, reminding me of my original question.

"They were all like you?" I asked.

"In a sense. Much like you and the other females of your species are the same, you are different."

"Okay," I said with a nod. "How did you

communicate with one another? I mean, space is massive. It took us humans nearly a decade to reach Ankau…if our records are correct."

"They are," he said. Good to know. *"My kin and I communicated much as you and I communicate now. For us, the distance in space is nothing because our minds are connected. When one wishes to speak, we simply open our mind and speak."*

Wow. The ability to just do that. I wondered how it would be if humans could do the same.

"Interesting."

"What's interesting?" I asked.

"Your other wondered the same thing about mental communication."

He was talking about Takar. "I guess he and I are more alike than I thought," I said.

"That is why I helped the two of you share your dream."

"My…dream?" I asked.

"In a sense," he said.

Now I had to know. "Was that dream…mine? Did that mean that it's not real?"

"It was real."

"How? Did you give it to us?" I demanded.

I could hear him chuckle in my mind as I watched his form shake a bit. *"To answer your unasked question, the dream you shared with Takar was something that showed a potential future. The connection between the two of you was stronger than I had felt in quite some time."*

"What do you mean, 'connection'?" I asked.

"Every being has a certain...what is the word you humans use...aura, or force about them. Perhaps it is more simplistic than that. There is a cosmic thread, connecting every being in the universe to another. Each of those threads vary in strength, some are as thin and tenuous as air, some are as strong as the forces that bring life into existence. You and Takar have one of those connections."

"We do?"

Puppet Master actually nodded.

"Then, what about the rest of your kind?" I asked, trying to force the conversation back on track. I wanted to know more about how he knew about Takar and me, but first things first.

He chuckled. *"You humans have such complex minds, a veritable web of tangents and directions for your thoughts to take. Before I answer your voiced question, let me finish with the other. The dream that the two of you shared was because I temporarily connected your minds and showed you what should come in your future. The two of you belong together. That is why you had such strong feelings for one another from the very beginning, even if you gave them the wrong meaning.*

"As to your voiced question, there used to be many of us stretched throughout the universe. Now, I am no longer sure.

I have not been in contact with them in thousands of your years."

"Why not?" I asked.

"I do not know. Our connections simply...vanished. The threads are still there, but my mind tells me that they are no longer connected."

That was worrisome. There was potential that he was the last one left, or that the others had abandoned him for some reason. I wondered if there was something I could do to help him, but then realized that there most likely wasn't. How was I supposed to find more of PM's kind if I didn't even know what *he* was?

Ooh. "Have you always been inside a planet?" I asked.

"No."

Really? Okay. "Oh, then...how are you inside one now?" I asked.

There was a moment's hesitation. *"When I first arrived in this,"* I felt some subconscious massaging of my mind, *"galaxy,"* he said after that small hesitation, *"I felt the comfortable heat of the sun and decided to bask in its warmth. During the millennia in which I slept, the dust and debris of the galaxy closed in around me and closed me in. When I awoke, I realized what had happened and decided to complete the creation. I spread myself throughout the earth, bringing it together properly and creating the atmosphere and plant life. A few hundred years later, a meteor shower struck, and the particles and enzymes eventually came together to form life."*

"And Ankau was born," I finished.

"Yes."

I nodded. Now I had a better understanding of things.

Sort of.

I doubted that all planets were made up of whatever kind of beings the Puppet Master was, but there were several, and something had messed with that.

He had said that it wasn't the Xathi, so what else could have severed the ties that Puppet Master had with his own kind?

And what were these cosmic threads that he said connected all of us together, and how did he 'see' them enough to see that Takar and I belonged together.

"That is something that I cannot answer with certainty. I simply have the ability to see the connections, much like you simply have the ability to understand science- related things better than others, or how Takar can learn things in a matter of hours or days when others need years. It is simply something that is."

"So, even though you're insanely old, you don't know everything. Is that what you're saying?" I asked.

"You are a very intelligent being for a speck of dust within the lifespan of time. Then again, my own life, which

makes yours seem to be less than an instant in comparison, is but a blip upon the timeline."

"Well, then," I said, noticing that all of my food was gone. "That's getting a bit deeper than I had anticipated. It's also time I get back to work or I'll get into trouble. Talk to you again?"

"I am always here, my friend."

I nodded, called Fen, and stepped through the rift back to work.

TAKAR

I felt better about my assignment today than I had previously, but I still wasn't enthusiastic about it.

I was back on desk duty listening to the humans of the city and neighboring small settlements voice their concerns and fears about what was happening. I tried to look at it as something that was required, a necessary evil of the job, and I was capable of pushing myself through the necessary evils. I just sincerely hated this particular evil.

I would rather face an entire squadron of Xathi hybrids with a stick than do this…a broken stick, made of wet paper, while both of my feet were chained together and that chain was being slowly drawn into a broken plasma coil that was overheating and ready to boil my innards.

With a deep breath and a sigh of resignation, I left the apartment and made my way to the office.

The streets were busier than usual this morning, but Daphne had told me something about some sort of holiday, so I guessed that was the reason for the extra foot traffic.

"Hey, you."

I turned to see Daphne jogging up behind me. "What are you doing here?" I asked as she caught up to me.

"Your brother told me where you were being assigned today," she chirped as she hopped up and kissed me on the cheek. "I figured I'd come help you out."

"Thank you," I said. "Are you sure, though? It's not the most interesting job around, you know."

"I know," she said. "But it is where I met you," she said coyly. "Maybe I'll meet a new guy there."

My jaw dropped, and she started laughing as she jogged away from me. "You know I'm teasing, right?" she called back to me. "I figured this morning would have shown you my feelings."

I…I had to shake my head. She had been around my brother far too much the past few days. That sick joke had Rokul's mark all over it.

"You know I'm going to make you pay for that,

right?" I teased. Then I started jogging towards her, letting a playful growl loose.

She screamed in mock terror, turned, and ran. I chased her down, caught her from behind, and swung her up in the air. Her scream echoed off the building, immediately followed by laughter from both of us. She reached back and brought my head down for a kiss. The passion in her kiss was a match for this morning.

Oh, skrell. I was becoming like my brother.

Not that I was arguing, just noticing.

"In all seriousness," I said as I set her down and started walking to the office, her hand dwarfed in my own. "Are you sure you want to do this? It's just a bunch of people complaining about things. Besides," I added before she could answer, "aren't you supposed to be at the hospital today?"

She shook her head. "Nope, day off."

"So, you're going to spend your day off sitting with me, listening to people complain about things?" I arched my eyebrow as I looked at her. "All day?"

She nodded. "Yep. Why? Don't you want me around?"

I squeezed her hand. "Of course, I want you around. Always," I said. "Just...this is not something that's going to be very fun."

"Eh," she shrugged. "As long as I'm sitting there with you, I'm good."

"Okay, if you insist," I said. "Just don't blame me if you get bored senseless, which is what I'm afraid is going to happen to me."

"You'll be fine," she said as she gave me a playful slap on the arm.

I didn't exactly believe her, but I did find myself feeling better about the day since she was with me. We walked into the building, said 'hello' to Tobias, who was smiling bigger than I had ever seen him smile before, and headed to the complaint office.

"Hold on," I said. I walked away from Daphne and back to Tobias. "Okay, what's with the big grin?"

He looked up from his desk, and I noticed the picture of him with the girl he had been interested in. I wished I remembered her name. "I wanted to thank you," he said. "Working with the general and his men has done wonders for my confidence."

"So, you two…" I pointed back and forth between the picture and him.

"Mm-hmm," he nodded. "And you won't believe this, but…" he looked around to see if anyone else was around, then motioned me in close. I leaned in. He whispered, "I asked her to marry me, without really thinking about it, and she said yes."

"She did?" I asked, standing straight, but whispering in return.

He nodded happily.

I stuck out my hand and he took it, shaking it vigorously. He had a nice firm grip. "Congratulations," I said. "I'm glad to see you happy."

"Thank you. I was scared to talk to her, and now..." he stopped talking. I didn't press him. He was happy. I patted him on the shoulder, and told him to send in the first person in five minutes. He nodded, looked at the picture and blew it a kiss, then returned to his work.

"What was that about?" Daphne asked me as I approached her.

"Not much," I said. "He just finally got over his fear and found a way to get what he wanted." I would let Tobias be the one to announce things, it wasn't my place.

"That's nice," she said. We entered the office, turned on the datapads and tablets, and got set up. The first person to come in looked a little confused when he saw the two of us, but when I directed him to sit, he didn't hesitate.

Like so many of these, there wasn't much I could do other than listen. He wanted to know how he was supposed to pay his workers at his farm if the crops continued to falter.

I explained to him that we were working on a way to ensure that no one suffered too much from this issue, and that there might be a chance we would be able to get things fixed before too long.

Which was, technically, true.

If what the general and the Puppet Master had spoken about, and what Daphne told me about her conversations with him, came to fruition, then the vegetation of the planet might soon be replenishing, returning to life.

Not that I told him any of the details. Still, he seemed satisfied with the answer and left. The next person to come in was a large man that, as soon as he saw me, scowled and asked if he could speak...and I quote...'with the human in the room, not some fruit-colored freak from outer space'.

Charming.

Daphne shrugged, and even though I wasn't terribly excited with the idea of leaving her alone, she'd holler if she needed me.

I stepped just outside the office, leaving the door cracked.

Just in case.

That first man wasn't the only one that day that didn't want to speak with me. I wasn't sure if it was because I was that intimidating due to my superior size, or if they were part of the 'anti-alien' group that still seemed to be growing.

During our shared lunch, Daphne tried to reassure me that it wasn't a big deal.

I wanted to agree with her, but I knew that it was

going to be an issue. If this group continued to grow, there would eventually be a confrontation. For now, things were quiet, but I could sense a growing discontent and unease that permeated the humans.

We spent the rest of the day listening to more people with complaints and concerns ranging from how much food there was, how were they going to pay their workers and how much longer before the rebuild effort made it to where the crash site was, to when we were leaving, how much longer before the aliens left, and would any of us 'sexy big men be interested in procreating with a *lot* of interested women…and a few men.'

Daphne laughed at that last one.

I…wasn't sure how to answer that one. I politely told them that I would look into it and ask if any of the others might be, but I also politely declined the invitation myself.

That evening, as we were walking home, I tried to figure out what our situation was with the humans. Many of them seemed accepting of us—some seemed a little more than 'accepting,' not counting the women that had joined with us—while there were some that hated us, deeply.

The hate was to be expected. We were different, unknown. The part that got me was that the ones that hated us seemed to be starting to become more brazen, more open in their hatred of us.

I looked down at Daphne as we walked, a smile on her face as she looked around at everything. The feeling that I had, looking at her, was that no matter who hated us, no matter who despised us and tried to push us away, as long as she wanted me, I would stay…for her.

She was my happy.

She was my home.

Why would I go anywhere else?

EPILOGUE: DAPHNE

I had always made fun of those girls that fell in love and moved in right after meeting a guy.

Now I'd gone and done the same thing. I just met this guy maybe a week ago. Wait, had it really only been a week?

Damn.

The girls I made fun of moved in after at least a few weeks, maybe a couple of months, and here I was, a week into a relationship, and we were already getting a place together.

But if I had to be honest with myself—none of those girls had ever gone through what Takar and I had gone through during our first week.

I mean, if you could find me a girl that had gone and lied to one of her best friends, tried to con an alien soldier out of information, snuck into the lair of an unknown creature, then met said unknown creature and learned that he was actually the life force behind the planet you were living on, and had a dream about the alien soldier you had first conned and learned that that dream was almost a prediction of your future together...then I wouldn't have made fun of her for moving in with him after only a week.

I might have worried about her sanity in other ways, though.

Since the odds of that exact scenario were as close to zero as you could get, I didn't think about it. Instead, after I had finished my shift at the hospital, and since Takar still had another hour left on his shift, I decided to walk across town to what some of the humans were starting to call Alien-HQ.

Yeah, humans are real creative. Glad I am one. Sarcasm aside, the situation building between the anti-alien groups and the *Vengeance* crew was going to come to a head, and soon.

There was no way around it.

Hell, one of the people I had been friends with at the hospital found out that I was with Takar and now she disliked me. Called me a traitor and everything. "How could you sleep with those alien bastards?" she had asked me this morning.

"I just got to know them. They're not as bad as you

think. They're actually pretty nice, in a soldier-y sort of way."

She rolled her eyes, let out a huff, and stormed out of the lab. I found out an hour later that she had put in for a transfer to Einhiv and cited me as the reason. "I can't work with an alien lover," she had told our boss.

That had hurt. Then I got over it. I decided that, if she didn't want to be around me just because I had a different opinion about someone, then it wasn't worth being around her either.

The rest of the day, I had thought about Takar and the Puppet Master, but mostly Takar. He was so gentle, it was completely opposite of how big he was. I knew of the phrase 'gentle giant,' but I had always thought it was just a way of trying to compliment someone for *not* breaking something.

But, with Takar—and by extension, his brother—I now knew that the phrase honestly meant something.

I looked around me as I walked the city streets. I could still see, if I looked east, the devastation of what had happened when the Xathi ship had crashed down and taken out nearly half the city. From what I heard, cleanup crews and construction teams were still finding bodies. It was…sad. However, if I looked in any of the other directions, the city was beautiful.

Birds chirped as they flew overhead. The weather was nice and cool, a slight breeze keeping the temperature perfect. Big fluffy clouds floated lazily in the blue sky while that same light breeze brought the smells of Food Lane to my nostrils.

That was what most of us called Rocher Street. Two bakeries, three restaurants, a couple of small cafes, and an herb shop made up most of the businesses on the street, so when the wind blew in the right direction, the smells filled the air and always made me hungry. It was a wonder I wasn't four-hundred pounds, it all smelled so good.

I decided to bypass Rocher Street and head through the park instead. It was a beautiful day, why not enjoy the nature that the Puppet Master was trying to save? I really loved the park, even more so now that I knew what the park was really made of.

I picked up a plastic bottle from the pathway, dropped it off in one of the recycling bins, and went to go sit on one of the benches near the pond. The two fountains that had been placed in the pond sprayed their water up and out, and with the breeze, an invigorating mist of cool water hit me.

I sat back and relaxed, closing my eyes and enjoying the mist and the shade of the tree the bench was under.

"Should I just let you sleep here or carry you home?"

I didn't open my eyes. I didn't need to. There was no mistaking Takar's voice, or his sass now that we were comfortable with each other.

"I'll be honest with you," I said with a smile. "Between the mist coming with the breeze and the cool temperature, I wouldn't mind sleeping under the sky tonight." I opened my eyes to see Takar, his muscles, and his smile looking down at me. "Wanna join me?"

He gave me a one-shoulder shrug. "Wherever you are, I'll be happy there with you." It was a cheesy line, but my heart fluttered when he said it because I knew he meant it. I felt the same way, another something I would have normally laughed at those girls for.

"But," he said, almost ruining the moment, "we do have our new place to go to, unless you want to tell that house-seller that we're no longer interested."

"Okay, okay," I said, playfully complaining. "Geez, can't a girl just enjoy the weather? We were underground for forever," I joked.

He shook his head. "You know very well we were down there just over half a day." I wasn't sure if he was sassing me again, or if he was being serious. I decided to take it as a sassy moment.

"Okay, fine. Let's go to our house." I stood up and hooked my arm through his, then laid my head against his arm as we walked. It felt incredible to say *'our house.'*

We didn't have far to walk, we were actually only a few houses down from one of Takar's teammate's, and I loved our place. We had decided to get it based on what we had been shown in our shared dream, so we had a four-bedroom house, that way each of our kids…when we had them…would have their own room.

Was that a crazy way to go house shopping? Probably.

Was it any crazier than the way we got together?

Nope.

Besides, the bedroom and bathroom from the dream were an exact match for the bedroom and bathroom in this house. It was too much of a coincidence for us to have passed it up.

We got the house, a beautiful two-story with attic and basement. The wraparound porch hugged the entire house, letting us be outside yet protected from the elements at the same time. The front yard already had beautiful flowers planted in the two small gardens, and the backyard was massive…and it had a fenced-off inground pool.

We climbed up the three stairs of the porch, and Takar pulled out the keys. "Would you like to do the honors?" he asked me, holding the keys out to me. I smiled as I took the keys, put the key in the lock, and opened up our house.

Our house, it feels good.

I pushed the door open and immediately let out a gasp. Inside, tiny little flowers and plants were everywhere. The floor, which had been smooth planks of wood, was now covered by a thick ankle-height layer of grass.

"What in the zet is this?" Takar cursed behind me.

I took a step inside, Takar right behind me. As we stepped, slowly, into the middle of the room, I noticed that the flowers almost seemed to follow us. "Oh, my god." I whispered, my hand to my mouth. "I know what this is."

"What?"

"It's the Puppet Master's gift to us," I answered, looking up at Takar. "He made the house beautiful for us."

"You're okay with this?" he asked, looking around, then stopping to stare at a corner of what we had planned to use as the dining room.

I looked over and stared at what he was looking at. It was a small tree with what looked like both Terran apples and oranges hanging off its branches. In another corner was something like a lemon tree, and a peach tree stood in a third corner.

"Guess he remembered I like fruit," I quipped.

Takar nodded. At that moment that I saw his anger leave, almost as if he liked having nature inside the house. "I guess we could live with it. I just wish he hadn't messed with the floors. They were my favorite part of the house," he said.

As soon as he was done saying it, the grass receded,

disappearing through the microscopic gaps between each floor board. We looked at one another, eyes wide. "Well…that's different," I said. He merely nodded.

I loved the house, and I spent the next hour convincing him that it was nice to have living plants in the home. They cleaned the air, they brightened people's moods, it was a good thing.

To be honest, though, I think it was the fruit trees that sold him. He had already polished off two oranges and a peach.

It was beautiful.

Stroking one of the vines, I silently thanked Puppet Master for his gift to us. He was an amazing being, and that made me worry about him.

What had happened to his kin? What if they had been killed? What if they came for us?

But all of those concerns faded as I caught Takar sniffing some of the flowers.

You know what?

As long as I always had Takar in my life, I would have something to look forward to and enjoy.

And I fully planned on enjoying my time with him.

Starting with christening the house.

Every single room.

I mean, we *were* supposed to have kids, right?

LETTER FROM ELIN

Well, now we have some answers… and a few more questions!

Next in our main storyline is *Zarik,* something of a loner Skotan with something to prove… But before that, something we've all been waiting for.

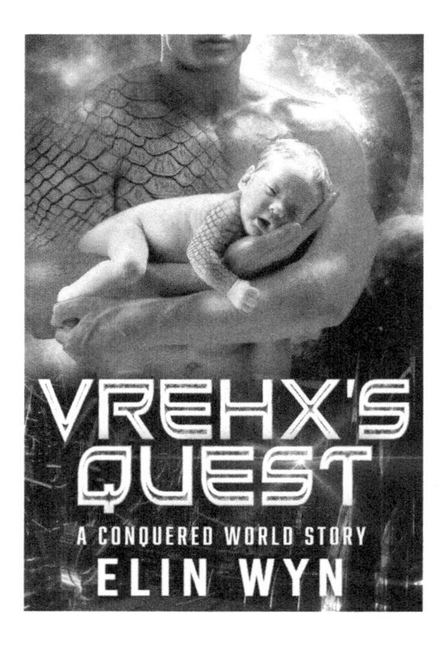

The wait is almost over. But is Vrehx ready for his biggest challenge yet?

Find Vrehx's Quest on Amazon!

And for more alien goodness, keep reading for a sneak peek of Zarik!

XOXO,

Elin

ZARIK: SNEAK PEEK

Miri

"The toxin will be even stronger than what those bastards have been using on us," I heard someone say.

I thrashed. The shadows in the blackness shifted. My body exploded with pain. Against my cheek was something sharp, maybe even spiky, but not at all durable. A crunching noise penetrated that awful ringing. An earthy smell invaded my senses.

The ringing sound began to dull, but it was replaced by an equally awful rushing in my ears. Something brushed against my cheek. My face twitched. Even that ached. My eyelids fluttered painfully.

I realized I wasn't in a sea of blackness at all. My

eyes were closed to protect themselves from the blinding white light that surrounded me. At least I could trust my body to look after itself when I clearly couldn't.

Slowly, I opened my eyes. It was a slow and painful process.

Why did I hurt so much?

The white light was blinding at first, but as my eyes adjusted, I began to see distinct shapes within the blaze. Pale greens and yellows. A few scratching blinks revealed those shapes to be leaves and branches. I was in the forest.

What was I doing in the forest?

I tried to think back to what happened before I woke up here. Panic seized me when I searched for memories but found nothing but emptiness. It was as if I hadn't existed before this very moment.

I sucked a shuddering, dirt filled breath into my lungs. The air burned my throat. Coughs rattled my body so hard I feared my ribs would break.

Water. I needed water.

I gasped softly. I remembered what water was. That was something. Not much, but it was a sign that my mind wasn't completely blank.

As I lay there, I took inventory of the things I knew for certain. I was in a forest. There was dirt and dead leaves beneath me. Branches and verdant leaves above me. I assumed there were rocks and roots as well.

I needed to see more, see what else I remembered. I sucked in another breath and willed my body to work. I pushed myself up. Sharp, brittle leaves dug into my palms as I pushed myself up. Every joint and muscle cried out in protest.

Nausea rolled through me. The hollowness in my stomach told me there was nothing to retch up even if I'd wanted to.

My arms trembled under the weight of my upper body. I still couldn't get my legs to move.

I told myself my situation wasn't as dire as it had been a moment ago. I could see, I could breathe. My movement was limited, but I could move.

It occurred to me that I might have a broken bone somewhere. Ah, I could add bones to my list. And blood.

I breathed a small sigh of relief. Things were coming back to me. I just had to think about them for a moment. With great effort, I rolled myself onto my back and supported my upper body with my forearms. They ached and trembled but I now had a better vantage point of the world around me.

I looked at my legs. I was wearing pants, a thick, durable fabric with a choppy pattern that looked like it was modeled after the forest floor. There was an insignia on one of the side pockets, but I didn't recognize it.

Covering my torso was a different fabric, still durable but lighter in weight. It was deep blue. Another insignia was sewn into the sleeve. I didn't recognize that one either. The boots on my feet were scuffed from use and worn in certain spots.

Looking at the articles of clothing I wore, I didn't think they belonged to me. Just by looking at them, I could tell they didn't fit right.

The pants were too big. The shirt was tight around my shoulders. The boots looked big to me, but I wouldn't be able to tell for certain until I got up and moved around. Who knew when that would be?

Not I.

I slowly rotated one foot, testing for pain. There was muscle soreness but nothing unbearable. I rotated the other foot with the same results.

Ankle, muscle, sprain. I knew what those words meant.

I bent my legs at the knee and tried to push my weight onto my heels, but my body wasn't ready to cooperate. It was worn out. I looked around for a good place to rest. I didn't fancy laying back down on the forest floor.

Nearby was a thick tree trunk covered in soft looking moss that looked ideal. Relying on my arms more than anything, I pulled myself over to the tree trunk. I sat with my back against the moss. It wasn't as soft as it looked but it stopped the jagged tree bark from cutting into my sore back.

"Okay," I sighed and sharply drew in a breath. My own voice caught me off guard. I forgot I could speak. My throat was dry and scratchy, but I tried to speak again. "Let's try to think about this."

All around me was the forest. It would've been too lucky if there was some kind of sign nearby. But if there had been a sign, would I have been able to read it? Would I recognize the name?

My mouth dropped open in horror as I came to a realization. Could I remember my own name?

No.

What was I going to do if I didn't know my own name? No one would be able to help me if I couldn't tell them who I was.

I closed my eyes. Shutting out the world around me might help me think.

I pictured my own face, an initially difficult task. I knew my hair was dark. I had the strange sense that it was long, but when I touched my hair, I found it cropped at the chin. I moved on to the shape of my face. My cheeks felt gaunt. My lips were dry but full in shape. My nose was straight and unremarkable.

I couldn't remember what color my eyes were.

A sea of faces that might've had my features swam through my mind. I flipped through them like an old picture book. A memory slipped in between the fabricated faces. A reflection in a cracked mirror. It was me. I looked scared. The rest of the memory fragments clicked into place. I'd just broken the mirror by accident. The mirror was important for some reason. Perhaps it was very old. My mother was going to be furious when she found out.

"Miri!" The voice in the memory shouted just before the memory faded away completely.

Miri.

That was my name.

"Miri." I tested the syllables as if that would give me some kind of confirmation.

What now?

I remembered the forest as a vast and dangerous place. I assumed the odds of someone stumbling across me here were slim. I stood a better chance if I somehow figured out where I was and going from there.

I closed my eyes again, hoping to call up another useful half-memory. I saw flashes of a city street. For a split second, I smelled fried corn cakes from a street vendor. I squeezed my eyes shut tighter in an attempt to bring the memory into clearer focus.

I saw the wrinkled face of the street vendor. He

smiled and thrust a corncake into my unexpecting hands. I tried to give him money, but he refused.

The corn cake was sweeter than I expected. The vendor must've glazed it with honey.

This memory was pleasant, but not helpful. It faded away like smoke before I could think of anything useful. Surely, I knew the name of that city. I clearly knew the street vendor.

A name struggled to take form on my lips.

Kluster. No, that wasn't right. Kanter. No.

Kaster.

The name clicked into place with the memory. That street vendor was from Kaster. Was I from Kaster?

I tried to dig up another memory, but nothing came up. All I knew for sure was that at some point, I'd made friends with a street vendor in Kaster. But where was Kaster?

I squeezed my eyes shut and concentrated until pressure throbbed between my eyes. Looking for my locked memories felt like trying to empty an ocean with a cracked bucket.

Another name surfaced after some time.

Duvest. I was pretty sure it was another city. Was it near Kaster? More importantly, was I near either of those places? Even if my memory was perfectly intact, figuring out where I was would be a challenge. Nothing in my surroundings gave me a clue.

With a long, tired sigh I let my head rest against the tree trunk. I decided I wasn't going to worry about where I was right now. Until I started to remember more, there wasn't much I could do. Besides, my body was exhausted. Whatever had happened to me took a serious toll.

Perhaps, I simply needed some sleep. My eyelids were already drooping.

Yes, just a few moments of sleep and I would wake up feeling much better.

Right?

Zarik

Do you know what one of the biggest benefits is to essentially being invisible?

You basically get to do what you want without getting into too much trouble for it.

The other big benefit?

People say things around you they normally wouldn't because they don't remember or notice that you're there.

In my case, being invisible had its advantages before the *Vengeance* was destroyed. I used to collect things, things that most of the rest of the crew thought were unusual, disgusting, or downright weird.

And that was fine. I enjoyed my collection, and my solitude. It wasn't like I had earned or deserved people's attention.

Now, before the ship blew up, I was Zairk—second engineer. Rouhr had brought me on board and given me an opportunity to prove myself and regain my honor.

Another one of the benefits of no one ever paying attention to you was that you generally heard many things that wouldn't normally be said while you were around.

Such as—today, when I had been walking behind General Rouhr, Strike Team Commander Karzin, Strike Team Commander Sk'lar, and two of the human guards, they were speaking of a woman that had come in earlier that day, distressed about her missing daughter.

Curious, I followed Karzin and Sk'lar as they headed out to the room where the woman was, ready to file a missing person report.

With a datapad in his hand, Karzin looked more bored than interested on the whole situation.

"Mind if I join you?" I asked them right before we stepped inside the cramped interrogation room. Sk'lar looked back at me over his shoulder, eyebrows shooting up as if only now he was realizing I had been following him, and exchanged a glance with Karzin before shrugging.

"Suit yourself," he said. "This is probably nothing."

Following after him, I stepped inside the room and took a seat across the middle-aged woman. She had deep wrinkles around her eyes, wrinkles that seemed even deeper in her distress, and a few locks of white hair had already started to take over her brown hair. In a room that was nothing but three bare walls and a one-way mirror, she looked even smaller in stature than she really was.

"Finally," she cried out, nervously running her tongue over her lips. "I've been waiting here for almost an hour."

"I'm sorry, ma'am," Karzin said, his tone polite. "Busy day."

"I understand that, but I'd like to see some effort being put into looking for my daughter."

"Ma'am, I can assure you...the city officials are already doing the best they—"

"That's bullshit," she cut him short, her lips tightly pursed. "I know they haven't even looked for her outside the city, or even in the ruins. That's why I've come here. I need *your* help."

"Very well," Karzin sighed, flipping his padd open and readying for some notes. "What can you tell me about your daughters? And when was the last time you saw her?"

His pen flew across the paper quickly as the woman spoke, but just one glance at the padd and I could see he wasn't taking notes of everything.

Just the basics, the outline.

That was unlike him.

Karzin had always prided himself on a job well done, so I never thought he'd be the kind of commander to do things in a lackadaisical manner.

"Right, I think we have everything we need," he finally said when the woman was done with her story. "I'll see what we can do about it, and we'll be in touch."

"Thank you," she breathed out, looking more relieved now. As for me, my curiosity had turned into perplexity. The moment Karzin, Sk'lar and I left the room, I couldn't help but stop them.

"What was that about?"

"What do you mean?"

"You didn't seem particularly concerned in there," I replied, doing my best not to accuse them of negligence. "Almost as if you didn't believe her."

"It's not that," Karzin shrugged. "Do you have any idea how many missing reports I've had to file these past few weeks? Communication between cities is spotty at best, and the war has brought on mass migration. Most people have just up and left without telling their families about it."

His jaw tightened. I knew, we all knew, how he felt about family. About losing family. This had be be harder on him than I realized.

He took a deep breath and continued. "Some see it as an opportunity for a fresh start, or they just want to run away from it all. The way I see it, this woman's daughter just got a new job somewhere and left to do it. I've noticed that many of these humans don't even speak to their family for many days, even though they are in the same place. This girl has probably just gone off and forgotten to say something about it. We shouldn't waste the resources."

Sk'lar, surprisingly, had been inclined to agree with Karzin...not about the girl's lack of compassion and common sense to speak to her mother, but about not wasting resources looking for her.

That wasn't a huge surprise. K'ver in general were known for their logic. And Sk'lar in particular had a reputation for putting practical concerns first.

And last.

"We have enough to deal with with these anti-alien factions that are spreading their filth around the city and other towns. I say we send one or two people out to look for her for a day, then go back to dealing with what is right in front of our faces. If this is a problem, surely the human guards can take care of it."

"Understood," I merely nodded, already thinking.

Predictably, the General listened, but disagreed.

The two human guards, both Lieutenants for the city if I read their rankings correctly, disagreed with one another. One of the them, the fat one, agreed with Karzin and Sk'lar. The other felt that it was our duty to investigate.

It was the other one that I agreed with.

And still, it wasn't my place to say anything.

Yet.

I went down to my room and sat, hunched at my desk. Despite Tobias' efforts find me a proper chair, he had been unable to find one that allowed for my considerable height.

However, discomfort did not bother me.

It was merely something to be endured.

I quickly got into the database and began my search for the file that the city officials had undoubtedly created. As surly as Karzin still was, despite his connection to a human female, he was a stickler for files.

Even if he'd decided that there was little we could do, I was betting he'd have found the report by the city officials, attached it to his own.

He created and kept files about everything. And, as suspected, there was a file about the missing woman.

Opening the file, I read the report, which was detailed, and wondered how he could simply throw this situation to the wayside.

Perhaps he'd found the report, but not bothered to read it. It was the only explanation.

The woman in question had strong ties to the city. She had been a volunteer in the cleanup process as well as at one of the local food banks.

None of her neighbors, co-workers, or friends remembered anything about her saying that she would be leaving. According to statements taken by the city guard that had investigated, she had left the city only three times during her life, and one of those was during the invasion.

As a matter of fact, the last she had been seen by anyone was on Seyka Street heading to her work.

How Karzin could possibly feel that this woman had simply taken a new job somewhere, or had simply gone somewhere without telling her mother or her friends?

They must have simply looked at the beginnings of the file when the mother came in and assumed things.

Very well, if they were unwilling to look into this, then I would.

It wouldn't be wasting valuable resources.

I wasn't a resource. I was invisible. Unnoticed.

Most importantly, perhaps this would be a way for me to begin to restoring my honor.

And for that, I'd do anything.

Miri

I STUMBLED through the forest in a daze, tree branches whipping my arms with every step I took. With no idea of where I was going, I didn't even know if I was venturing out of the forest or further into it, but I didn't even care.

All I knew was that I had to keep walking.

Easier said than done, of course. I was growing weaker with each passing minute, my stomach roiling audibly: I was so hungry that I could eat the bark off a tree. I stopped for a minute then, one hand on a tree trunk as I tried to catch my breath.

My body was soaked with sweat, locks of greasy hair plastered on my forehead, and my muscles felt as heavy as lead.

"Yes, please," I muttered under my breath, noticing an overgrown thorny bush just a few feet away from me. Red berries weighed down its thin branches, and I landed on my knees as I started picking them up eagerly. I stopped when I had a handful, my hands shaking from how weak I was, but I hesitated before putting any of the berries into my mouth.

Were the berries even edible? Or could they be poisonous?

I tried to rack my brains for an answer but there was nothing. Either I had never known about wild berries, or I simply couldn't remember. "Great," I groaned, opening my hand and allowing the berries to spill onto the ground.

I watched them roll away from me with a heavy heart, and for a moment I even thought of taking the risk and eating them anyway.

I didn't. As hungry as I was, I wasn't looking forward to poison myself and risk a slow painful death in the middle of nowhere.

Groaning, I pushed myself up to my feet and dusted my pants off. I scanned my surroundings once more, praying for my memories to return, but I found nothing but the echo of my own thoughts inside my head.

The only thing I had was a name—Miri—but that was as useful as a good behavior badge during trench warfare. In fact, I would be much happier if I didn't know my name and, instead, knew how to distinguish edible berries from poisonous ones.

"Just keep walking," I told myself, frowning at the sound of my own voice. It sounded strange and familiar at the same time, which made for a really unsettling experience.

I decided to keep my mouth shut as I walked, knowing that it'd be of no use to obsess about who I was...or used to be. The important thing was to find a way back into civilization. If I had any luck, there'd be some kind of city or town nearby.

Of course, I could also be stranded in the middle of nowhere, no other human being for miles in each direction.

Thankfully, it just took me a couple of hours before I stumbled in what seemed like a small outpost. Still a few hundred feet away from its outer walls, the thick vegetation keeping me hidden from sight, I took a moment to examine it.

The walls were small despite their sturdy appearance, and I could see a dozen squat buildings right behind them. There didn't seem to be much activity going on, but it was better than nothing.

Only when I started walking toward the outpost did I realize there were guards posted on the main gate. There were just two of them, and they were casually talking between themselves, their guns holstered. Even though I didn't like the idea of talking with someone that could potentially shoot, I had no other choice but to keep on walking toward them. They had already seen me, after all, and one of them was even pointing his finger straight at me.

"Good morning," one of them greeted me, and I was about to reply when I noticed there was something odd about the guards.

Not just odd.

Wrong.

They were much taller than a regular human, and their muscular bodies looked as if they had been designed to intimidate.

They wore full body armor that almost entirely covered their skin, with secondary plates.

Wait.

That wasn't body armor.

That was their skin.

And it was *green*.

These weren't humans...they were aliens.

I froze in place, not knowing what to think, and the two guards exchanged a confused glance. They started walking toward me and I couldn't stop myself from panicking.

"Stand back!" I cried out.

Where the hell was I? And why were freaking aliens in here?

I knew there was an answer for all those questions buried deep in my mind, but I couldn't dig it out fast enough. Especially with two green and scary looking giants making their way toward me.

"Calm down, miss," they continued to say, their deep voices making my heart beat even faster. Could I even trust them?

I was still trying to calm myself down when I realized they were walking away from each other, trying to flank me. They seemed hesitant about me, and that definitely didn't make me relax.

Before I even knew what I was doing, I had already launched myself forward and was running past them. They called after me but that just made run even faster, my feet kicking dust off the ground as I went.

I dashed into the small outpost in a panic, but I breathed out with relief as I realized there were humans inside the walls. A few threw curious glances my way, but most of them didn't even pay me any attention and just carried on with their normal lives.

"Come back here, miss!" The alien guards shouted from behind me. Looking back over my shoulder, I realized they were closing in on me and decided to keep on running.

No way was I going to let these two lay their hands on me, that was for sure. I was still glancing back at them, clearly not paying enough attention to what was in front of me, when I hit something and tumbled into the ground.

"Crap," I groaned, wincing as pain shot up from my knee to my thigh. There was a small overturned cart in front of me, a few jars of herbs and spices littering the ground, and all of it seemed to belong to a small elderly woman that was looking at me with an expression of pure confusion.

"What's wrong with you?" One of the guards frowned, the two of them now looking down on me. Great, I had been caught. "Why the hell are you running away from us?"

"Because...you're aliens"? I tried, not sure on what else they were expecting me to say.

"So?" One of them asked.

"She's probably a member of an anti-alien group," the other scoffed, folding his arms over his chest as he eyed me disapprovingly.

"I don't even know what you're talking about," I said meekly, looking at the elderly woman beside me and hoping for some support.

Her eyes jumped from me to the aliens, and then went back to me again. She seemed as confused as me and the aliens were.

"Do you know this woman, Kanna?" The guard closest to me asked the old woman. She shook her head and pursed her lips, her eyes never leaving mine. Slowly, she then went down on one knee and offered me a smile, locks of white hair tumbling over her shoulders.

"My name's Kanna," she said gently. "I'm this settlement's herbalist. Do you have a name?"

"Miri," I replied.

"Good. And how can we help you, Miri? You look a lil' bit lost, if I may say so," she continued, the kindness on her voice enough to make me feel more at ease. "Where have you come from?"

"The woods," I said, quickly glancing back to the place where I had just come from. Frowning, Kanna just eyed me for a short moment, her focus on the small cuts and bruises on my arms.

"And before the woods?"

"I...I don't know," I admitted, feeling a knot in my throat. Why couldn't I remember anything? There were so many questions bouncing around inside my head, and I felt that the answers were there too...but somehow they remained beyond my grasp. "I don't remember anything."

"You don't remember?" One of the guards asked, both his eyebrows arched.

"I don't. I just remember running through the woods..."

"Alright, sweetie," Kanna said, rising to her feet and offering me her hand. I took it, allowing the old woman to help me up. "Come with me into my shop, will you?

I'll get you something to eat and drink, and these two gentleman will try to figure something out."

I was too confused to protest. The aliens didn't seem hostile, and even Kanna seemed to trust them.

Besides, the important thing was that she had offered me food. At that point, I was hungry enough to follow whoever promised me a handful of breadcrumbs.

"And what are we supposed to do?" The guards asked Kanna, both of them looking uncomfortable. They seemed more prepared to deal with situations that required the use of a gun than with mysterious girls that didn't remember absolutely anything.

"Don't you have superiors?" Kanna told them sternly. "Get one of them on those comms of yours and tell them what's going. There has to be someone in the city capable of helping her."

"Right," one of them said, clearing his throat. "Of course."

"Now, let me just pick these things up and we'll go," she started, bending over to pick the jars of herbs I had knocked over. I helped her do it, feeling embarrassed about the whole situation, and then we were on our way.

"These two aren't the smartest of them," she said as we left the guards behind. "But they mean well."

"Yes, but..."

"But?"

"They are aliens!" I said, keeping my voice low so that no one could hear us.

"Why, of course they are," Kanna laughed. "Where have you been living all this time? Under a rock?"

"I have absolutely no idea," I said.

And that was the truth.

PLEASE DON'T FORGET TO LEAVE A REVIEW!

Readers rely on your opinions, and your review can help others decide on what books they read. Make sure your opinion is heard and leave a review where you purchased this book!

Don't miss a new release! You can sign up for release alerts at both Amazon and Bookbub:

bookbub.com/authors/elin-wyn

amazon.com/author/elinwyn

For a free short story, opportunities for advance review copies, release news and the occasional cat picture, please join the newsletter!

https://elinwynbooks.com/newsletter-signup/

And don't forget the Facebook group, where I post sneak peeks of chapters and covers!

https://www.facebook.com/groups/ElinWyn/

DON'T MISS THE STAR BREED!

Given: Star Breed Book One

When a renegade thief and a genetically enhanced mercenary collide, space gets a whole lot hotter!

Thief Kara Shimsi has learned three lessons well - keep her head down, her fingers light, and her tithes to the syndicate paid on time.

But now a failed heist has earned her a death sentence - a one-way ticket to the toxic Waste outside the dome. Her only chance is a deal with the syndicate's most ruthless enforcer, a wolfish mountain of genetically-modified muscle named Davien.

The thought makes her body tingle with dread-or is it heat?

Mercenary Davien has one focus: do whatever is necessary to get the credits to get off this backwater mining colony and back into space. The last thing he wants is a smart-mouthed thief - even if she does have the clue he needs to hunt down whoever attacked the floating lab he and his created brothers called home.

Caring is a liability. Desire is a commodity. And love could get you killed.

https://elinwynbooks.com/star-breed/

ABOUT THE AUTHOR

I love old movies – *To Catch a Thief, Notorious, All About Eve* — and anything with Katherine Hepburn in it. Clever, elegant people doing clever, elegant things.

I'm a hopeless romantic.

And I love science fiction and the promise of space.

So it makes perfect sense to me to try to merge all of those loves into a new science fiction world, where dashing heroes and lovely ladies have adventures, get into trouble, and find their true love in the stars!